'*Anything* would be George,' declares N rejects her only cha future.

High ideals may be fine in theory, but, as she soon discovers, alone and destitute in Victorian London, in real life one also needs things like food and shelter! And that is why she agrees to marry Lord Rutherford—a man she knows nothing about, except that he seems burdened by some terrible secret. Can she ever hope to understand such an enigmatic stranger? And dare she hope that he will one day come to love her?

LORD RUTHERFORD'S AFFAIR

JASMINE CRESSWELL

MILLS & BOON LIMITED
London · Sydney · Toronto

First published in Great Britain 1984
by Mills & Boon Limited, 15–16 Brook's Mews,
London W1A 1DR

© Jasmine Cresswell 1984
Australian copyright 1984
Philippine copyright 1984

ISBN 0 263 74785 9

Set in 11 on 12 pt Linotron Times
04–0884–51,000

Photoset by Rowland Phototypesetting Ltd
Bury St Edmunds, Suffolk
Made and printed in Great Britain by
Cox & Wyman Ltd, Reading

To John,
his own book at last.
With love.

CHAPTER
ONE

IT WAS already dark when Deborah pushed open
the iron gate and walked along the short path to her
lodgings. She glanced up and saw Mrs Pritchard's
bulky shadow outlined behind the thick lace curtains of the parlour. She sighed, but although she
was close to exhaustion she held her head high and
took care not to drag her feet. She couldn't afford
to appear dispirited when her landlady was watching. I wonder what she'd do if I waved, Deborah
thought, and for a moment the weariness of her
face was lightened by a faint smile.

The narrow path was full of puddles and she
could feel the damp seeping in through the holes in
her shoes, creeping up her stockings, but she
ignored the uncomfortable squelching sensation
and the icy chill of her toes. She was used to wet feet
by now. The soles of her shoes had finally worn out
late last week and it had rained every day since: the
sort of dirty, penetrating drizzle that seemed typical of London in autumn. Perhaps it will be warm
tomorrow, she thought. Perhaps it will be sunny
and the air crisp, so that my clothes will dry out at
last and it won't matter that my shoes are full of
holes.

As soon as she recognised the foolish trend of her thoughts she tightened her fists angrily beneath the folds of her shabby cape. Why did she constantly indulge in such unrealistic daydreaming? Even now, even after the last two terrible months, she still hadn't learned to accept the grim realities of her situation. She wondered what lingering memory of childhood happiness tempted her to hope that tomorrow—the first day of October—the clouds would roll away and reveal the brightness of a smiling sun and the brilliant blue of a perfect summer sky.

The delicate curve of her mouth suddenly straightened into a firm line. It was a long time since she had romped through the endless hot days of a Mediterranean summer, a long time since she had basked in the love of her devoted parents. She ought to be cured of wishful thinking by now. Eighteen months of living on Cousin George's cold charity, followed by two months of unsuccessful job-hunting in London, were harsh enough lessons to cure the most determined optimist.

With a quick shrug, Deborah unlocked the front door and stepped into the gloomy little lobby of the lodging-house. She wasn't surprised to find that Mrs Pritchard had already come out of her parlour and was waiting in the hall. With the infallible instincts of a seasoned landlady, she had sensed the desperation that pushed ever closer to the surface of Deborah's outward calm. The landlady had greeted her return every afternoon this week, never failing to drop a reminder that on Friday the next month's rent would fall due.

Deborah knew that any appeal for a few days' grace would be a waste of time. Mrs Pritchard prided herself on the fact that none of her boarders had ever managed to sneak even a single hour of unpaid lodging.

'I run a high-class commercial establishment, not a charitable institution,' she remarked frequently, clasping her hands in front of her ample, black-draped stomach, and resting her chin neatly on the shelf of her bosom. 'I take in only the most respectable ladies and gentlemen, and respectable people can *always* pay the rent. If they can't pay the rent, then they're not respectable, are they?' Mrs Pritchard was so well-satisfied with the circular logic of her reasoning that she ought to have appeared ridiculous, but Deborah found herself unable to laugh at the landlady's absurdities. She had learned to fear the implacable authority represented by Mrs Pritchard's folded hands and thin, pinched nostrils.

'Good evening, Miss Phipps.' Mrs Pritchard's pale eyes roamed over Deborah's bedraggled appearance in a swift, calculating sweep. 'You should have taken your umbrella,' she said. 'I can see you're soaked to the skin.'

She knows very well that I've had to sell my umbrella, Deborah thought, and a burst of stubborn pride enabled her to meet the landlady's gaze without a visible tremor. 'Good evening, Mrs Pritchard. Yes, indeed, it was foolish of me to forget my umbrella. I shall not make the same mistake tomorrow.'

'The pretty ribbons on your bonnet are all

ruined, and they are so costly to replace. I fear your
bonnet will never be the same after the soaking it
has received.' Mrs Pritchard's eyes gleamed with
malicious pleasure.

With considerable difficulty, Deborah managed
to hold her polite smile in place. 'Well, I shall have
to see about replacing the ribbons. It is an incon-
venience, Mrs Pritchard, but not a tragedy. The
London stores, after all, are full of pretty hat-
trimmings. There is no need for you to look so
concerned on my behalf.'

Mrs Pritchard's nostrils turned alarmingly white
and her lips snapped together in an angry down-
ward curve. She liked her victims to be suitably
cowed when she tormented them, and Miss Phipps
had repeatedly proved to be a very unsatisfactory
victim. The landlady's voice was hard with suppressed annoyance when she spoke again. 'I must
remind you, Miss Phipps, that tomorrow is the first
day of October.'

Deborah swallowed, unable to speak over the
lump of terror that constricted her throat. She was
grateful for the thick woollen folds of her cape,
which helped to conceal the shaking of her body.
She pressed her hands hard against her ribcage to
stop them from trembling. 'I am aware of the date,
Mrs Pritchard,' she said, doing her best to keep her
voice low and even.

'Then I am confident we need say no more. I am
quite sure we understand one another.' The landlady turned towards her parlour door, the black
bulk of her bombasine dress indefinably threaten-
ing in the narrow confines of the hall.

'No, please wait! Mrs Pritchard, there is something I must tell you . . . something I must ask . . .'

'Yes, Miss Phipps?'

'About the rent . . .'

Mrs Pritchard's narrow mouth relaxed into a tiny smile of satisfaction. So her instincts had not been at fault after all! She turned round quickly, her thick fingers spread out triumphantly against the corseted mound of her stomach. 'You know my rules, Miss Phipps,' she said, gloating over the words. 'This is a first-class boarding-house for ladies and gentlemen of the highest respectability. And respectable people are always punctual in paying their debts. They would never be so vulgar as to request an extension of time in meeting their obligations.'

Some insane demon of pride, the cursed monster that had propelled her to London in the first place, burst out of the confines where Deborah had struggled to contain it. 'You are quite mistaken, Mrs Pritchard,' she said coldly. 'I intended merely to inform you that I no longer require your room.'

'No longer require it? Well, Miss Phipps, I think you'll soon find out that there aren't any lodgings in London which are higher-class and more respectable than mine. Perhaps, however, you find it necessary to remove somewhere a little cheaper?'

'Once again you mistake the matter, Mrs Pritchard. I am leaving because . . . because . . .' Deborah paused while she sought wildly for some reason that was sufficiently impressive to stun even Mrs Pritchard into temporary silence. None sprang

to mind. Her brain remained obstinately and de-
vastatingly blank.

'Yes, Miss Phipps? And why is it exactly that you
are leaving?'

'I am leaving because . . . because I am to be
married.' The lie slipped trippingly from her
tongue, shocking Deborah at least as much as her
landlady.

'M-married?' Mrs Pritchard stuttered.

'Yes,' Deborah replied, momentarily delighted
with the success of her story. She expanded ruthlessly on the lie. 'It is a most advantageous match,'
she said, keeping her eyes lowered with a becoming
imitation of modesty. 'Naturally I am flattered . . .
honoured . . . that I have been chosen. My fiancé
is a nobleman, you know. A gentleman of the
first rank. You will be reading the announcement
shortly.'

Mrs Pritchard's bosom heaved dramatically. She
did not approve of lodgers who had too much good
fortune. 'This is most unexpected, Miss Phipps.
Most unexpected.'

'To you, perhaps, but not to me.' Deborah took
especial delight in smiling at her landlady with
marked condescension. 'Now, if you don't mind,
Mrs Pritchard, I will wish you good evening. You
will appreciate that I have a great many tasks to
complete tonight.'

'Oh yes, yes of course. Good evening to you,
Miss Phipps.' Mrs Pritchard did not attempt to
disguise her awe as her lodger swept along the
corridor in the direction of the steep, uncarpeted
stairway.

*   *   *

Deborah's brief feeling of elation did not survive the climb up three flights of stairs. She let herself into the tiny room that was hers for only one more night and flung her bonnet on to the bed. Mrs Pritchard was quite right, she noted dispassionately, the ribbons were utterly ruined.

'What a fool you are,' she whispered to her reflection in the narrow wall mirror. 'How could you have thrown away your only chance to keep a roof over your head? And simply because you were offended by the insufferable vulgarity of that woman? Will you never learn the futility of the grand gesture? Why could you not have inherited your mother's singing voice instead of her extravagant, impractical nature?'

She could find no satisfactory answer to her own questions. She unbuckled the fastenings of her cape, tossing it on to the bed alongside the ruined bonnet. Her only remaining bonnet. Every other hat had been sold so that she might continue to eat.

Her head began to ache with an intolerable, pounding force, and she pulled the pins out of her thick chestnut hair, shaking the heavy strands into loose curls around her shoulders in an effort to relieve the pain. She noted bitterly that an unremitting diet of bread, cheese and tea had not marred the magnolia perfection of her complexion, and the shadows beneath her eyes merely emphasised the deep blue depths of her gaze.

She turned away from the mirror, angry with the startling beauty it reflected. She sometimes thought that her outstanding looks were a curse God had inflicted upon her as punishment for the sinful pride and obstinacy of her character. She had been trying to evade the consequences of her beauty since long before her sixteenth birthday, but with very little success.

If she had been ugly, she thought, Cousin George would never have wished to marry her. He would never have kept her hidden from the eligible young men of the neighbourhood, nor would he have continued to force his suit once she had refused him. If she had been ugly, Cousin George would never have tried to impress her by giving her a personal tour of his factories. And then she would never have seen exactly how he made the money that kept them both in idle luxury . . .

She had read in the newspapers that the Civil War raging in America had decreased the flow of cotton into the Lancashire mills, but she hadn't realised the effect this shortage of raw cotton would have upon local employment. Cousin George, of course, was considerably more sophisticated and he had been quick to spot a potential profit. During their tour of his factories, he informed her proudly that his labour costs had decreased steadily over the previous two years, as desperate weavers competed for jobs in the few factories still operating at full steam.

Deborah didn't want to remember the sights and smells of those terrible torture-houses George called his cloth mills . . . the misshapen bodies of the women, the unnatural quiet of the tiny children, the men missing fingers, hands, even arms, cut off in the ceaseless clacking of the looms. Whatever happened to her in the future, she could never regret that she had been courageous enough to refuse to live on the profits of such ugly human misery.

At the moment, however, the awareness of moral superiority was not much consolation. She admitted to herself that she yearned for the easy comfort of her days in the big stone house, nestled at the edge of the Yorkshire moors. She could almost taste the buttered scones and the hot, fragrant tea that arrived in the drawing-room each afternoon promptly at four.

Utterly weary, Deborah sat on the hard, straight-backed chair which was the only seat in the room. She had spent the entire day in an exhausting search for work. She had given up her original hope of obtaining a genteel post as a governess or companion more than two weeks ago. She was too young, prospective employers informed her, and without adequate experience. So, for the past fourteen days, she had tramped the streets of central London, stopping in stores and small shops seeking employment. The answer was always the same. At nineteen, she was too old to become an apprentice, too inexperienced to be taken on as a saleslady, and not strong enough to work in a warehouse or cleaning up floors. The world, she decided tiredly, had no respectable place for an educated woman who lacked the good sense to get herself married off before she approached her twentieth birthday.

Deborah stared into the empty fire-grate, not even noticing that it was screened with a fresh sample of Mrs Pritchard's hand-painted paper fans. What was she going to do tomorrow? For the first time, she allowed herself to acknowledge the full extent of her fear. She was deeply and agonisingly frightened. Slowly she reached for the concealed pocket in her skirt and removed her soft leather purse from its hiding-place. She held it for a moment in the palm of her hand, not moving, delaying the time when she must pull open its flaps and count the contents, although she knew exactly what she would find inside: one shilling, a shiny sixpence, two pennies and five farthings. Nine coins of small denomination, and it was all that stood between her and destitution. About five days' worth of food, she estimated, if she could live on bread and water.

For a moment her eyes turned towards the uncurtained window, and she stared out into the darkness. Should she try to walk into the country? Was she strong enough to cover the necessary twelve or fifteen miles? Since she would have to sleep in the open air the following night, she might be safer away from town and the hardened criminals bred by London's intolerable poverty. 'Please God,' she murmured, 'let it be warm and dry tomorrow.'

The stark uncompromising fact of imminent starvation moved to the centre of her mind, blocking her capacity for constructive thought. Now, when she so desperately needed to come up with some rational plan for her future, her brain refused to co-operate, wandering off into the useless byways of childhood memory. She pulled her thoughts together with an almost physical effort. Perhaps there was something she could sell, something that would buy her accommodation while she

continued the search for work. She looked round
the bare room, but she didn't bother to get up from
the chair. She knew the search was meaningless, for
she no longer possessed anything other than the
clothes she wore and the bonnet and cape on the
bed.

There was nothing to hope for from Cousin
George. She had sunk her pride and written to him
last week, asking if she might come back. Even
now, she regretted the moment of hunger and
weakness that had tempted her to write. Her letter
had been returned unopened with a note from his
lawyer saying that, as far as Sir George Bellows was
concerned, Miss Deborah Phipps had ceased to
exist.

Deborah sprang to her feet, sending the chair
crashing to the floor. She didn't bother to pick it up
again. She quickly crossed the tiny room, halting
only inches away from the mirror.

'Well, you have one thing left to sell,' she said
defiantly. 'And God knows you have received
sufficient offers over the past two months.'

The pale image in the mirror blurred at the edges
and she dashed away a trickle of tears. 'Come,
come,' she told her reflection with a sudden harsh
laugh. 'Why are you crying? Is your memory so
short, my dear Deborah? Did you not declare, with
considerable dramatic vehemence, that *anything*
would be better than marrying Cousin George?'

There was still no answer from the pale girl in the
mirror, and Deborah turned away with an abrupt
gesture of revulsion. She walked to the window
pressing her forehead against the coolness of the

glass pane. The rain had stopped, she noticed, and the navy-blue sky sparkled with an elegant shimmer of stars.

Deborah drew in a deep breath. 'I will not starve,' she said through clenched teeth. 'I am not yet ready to die.' She pulled her hair back from her face, twisting it into a thick coil that she piled on top of her head, securing the heavy mass with a couple of pins. She clamped her wet bonnet somewhat precariously on top of this shaky mound, then draped her cloak around her shoulders.

When she paused by the door, she saw that the girl in the mirror was still watching her. For a moment, Deborah was frightened. The reflection seemed alien, separate from herself, a strange entity with a life of its own. She put her hands to her head, which felt curiously light and dizzy. 'I am going to eat,' she said, and it seemed perfectly right that she should justify her actions to a mere reflection. 'I am going to eat and eat until I don't feel hungry any more. I think I shall try a hot eel pie from the man who keeps the stall on Battersea Bridge.'

It seemed to Deborah that the girl in the mirror looked decidedly disapproving. 'I know eel pies aren't ladylike,' Deborah said rebelliously. 'But I dare say a woman who is preparing for a life of sin need not care about appearing ladylike.' She scowled at the silent mirror. 'I have quite made up my mind, so there is not a particle of use in looking down your nose at me.'

There was another long silence while she and the girl stared at each other. The silence made

Deborah acutely uncomfortable, until defiance once more took over.

'You may stare at me if you wish,' she said, 'but I shall have done worse than eat a few eel pies before this evening is over. I am going to buy spirituous liquor and then I am going to . . . I am going to . . .'

The outrage of the prim girl in the mirror was all too evident, and Deborah's spate of words dwindled into an unhappy silence. Perhaps, she decided, it would be more tactful if she didn't mention exactly what she planned to do when she had drunk a sufficient quantity of alcohol. As a matter of fact, although she was quite clear in her mind that she intended to become a Fallen Woman, she was not at all clear exactly what path she would have to pursue in order to achieve this sinful end. However, from everything she had ever heard, the purchase of spirits was definitely a step in the right direction.

Deborah turned round and once more looked angrily towards the reproachful girl. 'It's all very well for you to lecture me on the evils of drink,' she said. 'But you are not standing on my side of the mirror.'

She paused and thought for a moment about her last remark. There was definitely something wrong with it. The mirror was attached to the wall, so nobody was standing behind it. The throbbing in her head returned with renewed force, and she shook her head impatiently. There were other, more important, matters to consider at this precise moment. 'I am going to buy gin,' she said mutinously as she opened the door. 'I dare say I could buy a whole bottle of gin for a shilling and that leaves me ninepence farthing to spend on eel pies. At least tonight I shall not be hungry. *You* may keep your virtue and skulk behind that mirror if you choose.'

She shut the door, not waiting to hear what the other girl might care to say. Her head felt as though it might be floating somewhere a few inches above her body. She thought about the sensation for a moment and decided it was rather pleasant.

She ran swiftly down the steep stairs and escaped into the crisp darkness of the night. She could almost smell the warm steam of the pie stall, carried on a gentle breeze from the Thames. She could already taste the juicy richness of the eel pie. Deborah unlatched Mrs Pritchard's iron gate and, on light feet, hurried in the direction of Battersea Bridge.

CHAPTER
TWO

JOHN, LORD Rutherford arrived back at his town house in the early hours of the morning. He had left his club after midnight, waving away the porter's offer of a cab. He had then walked down St James's Street and cut across the park, deliberately taking the long way home. As he walked, he wrestled with the problem of his future, which seemed to become more intractable the more he thought about it.

He had started the evening by attending a dinner party at his mother's house and he had been appalled to find himself the object of much jocular speculation among his fellow guests. His mother's circle of friends, he discovered, waited in daily expectation of hearing that he had made an offer for Miss Celia Chalmley's hand. Lord Rutherford swung his slender cane impatiently as he walked along, searching his conscience, but he could think of nothing he had done which entitled society to leap to such a conclusion. He had always been so careful in his relationships with eligible young women, ever since he first learned the horrifying truth about how his father died.

He sighed. The family estates groaned under an increasing burden of debt, and the terms of his great-grandfather's will meant that he could touch no capital until he married. No wonder that his mother protested at his scruples and constantly schemed to throw prospective brides in his path.

But on this occasion she had clearly overstepped the limits of what he could tolerate. She must be made to understand that he would accept no further interference in the organisation of his life. It had been all too evident tonight that Celia Chalmley's family anticipated a proposal, something they could not rationally expect unless his mother had made rash, unjustifiable promises on his behalf.

He felt guilty about Celia Chalmley's false expectations. She seemed a thoroughly nice child, a little dull but basically sweet-natured. She didn't deserve to have her hopes raised in such a useless cause. Neither did she deserve to have her name bandied about at other people's dinner parties. As long as he remained single, however, there seemed to be no way of halting the endless speculation about his choice of wife. Nobody suspected the real reason why he remained a bachelor. The secret of his father's manner of death had been too well kept.

Lord Rutherford swore silently, with long and impressive fluency. *Damn* his mother, and her ceaseless, reckless, scheming! If she produced one more 'eligible' young girl for his inspection, he was likely to go quite mad. His mouth twisted into a bitter, ugly smile. Perhaps I should point that fact out to her, he thought. Shall I warn her that if she continues with her present tactics, my fate is likely to fall upon me sooner than either of us anticipates? Does she really want to see me, raving like my father, a minute sooner than she has to?

His concentration was so deep that he almost stumbled over the hunched body huddled against the railings in front of his house. He looked down at the pathetic figure without sympathy, his harsh features wrinkling into a faint frown of distaste. It was a woman, he decided. Her face was obscured by the collar of her grey cloak, but her drab skirts and battered bonnet, just visible above the cloak, proclaimed her sex. Even at this distance he could smell the stink of gin that soaked through her clothes and lingered unpleasantly in the night air.

He was tempted to leave her just where she was, but some trace of reluctant pity halted his footsteps as he made to walk round her. The sky had become heavily clouded during the last half-hour and it looked as if it might rain again at any minute. He supposed that he ought to reassure himself that she was capable of finding shelter. If she was a habitual drinker, a heavy rainstorm might easily give her a fatal congestion of the lungs.

He shook her impatiently, angry that she had been inconsiderate enough to collapse near his property, and equally angry with himself because he couldn't just walk over her and leave her to her fate.

He prodded the soggy mass of her cloak with the toe of one of his evening slippers, but this produced no reaction other than a low groan. Impatiently, he bent down and grabbed her by the shoulders, shaking her with an energy fuelled by his intense annoyance. He had sufficient problems of his own at the moment without undertaking the rescue of drunken layabouts. He gave the woman a final, violent shake.

'Would you pleash . . . please . . . go away? You are dishtur . . . distursh . . . You are bothering me.'

He was surprised by the soft, educated sound of her voice, although it was well known that some of the more highly-trained prostitutes and actresses could mimic the accents of the nobility with remarkable accuracy.

'I do beg your pardon,' he said with an irony which he knew must be lost on her. 'I apologise for disturbing you, but I would like to point out that the spot where you have chosen to doss down for the night happens to belong to me. I should also like to point out that it's going to rain at any minute and you are going to get wet.'

'Oh *fiddle*! It'sh *always* raining here.'

'A depressing fact of London life. I fear London is not a city noted for its sunny climate.'

Of course she made no reply to his mocking comments, and he suddenly tired of the one-sided game. 'You'd better move along to wherever you plan to pass the rest of the night,' he said roughly. 'If a policeman finds you here, you'll end up spending the night in gaol.'

'Dear, dear, Mrs Pritchard would never approve of *that*! Reshpecable ladies and gennelmen never go to gaol.' The woman's tiny gurgle of laughter was quickly smothered by a groan. 'I am getting up now,' she said. 'Don't rush me.' With considerable difficulty, she pulled herself to her feet, holding on to the railings for support.

Lord Rutherford watched her efforts in silence. He was surprised to find that his lips had curved into a shadow of a smile when he heard her ripple of laughter, and he admitted to himself that he felt a mild curiosity as to the chain of events that had brought this woman to the pavement outside his house. She undoubtedly had a colourful past, if she could ever be persuaded to tell the truth of it. Where had she learned to speak with such an aristocratic accent? Even the drunken slurring of her words couldn't disguise the basic perfection of her diction. He was puzzled by the startling contrast between her appearance—not to mention her smell—and her wonderfully melodious voice. But his brief moment of interest quickly passed, and his features returned to their habitual severity. There was no mystery, he thought. She was undoubtedly an actress, thrown out of work for repeated over-indulgence in gin.

The woman had meanwhile abandoned her effort to remain standing upright. After a few wobbly moments on her feet, she gave an angry little grunt and let go of the railings, slithering back into an inelegant heap on the pavement.

The last remnant of Lord Rutherford's curiosity disappeared in a flash of temper. Blast the woman, she was intolerably drunk! It was late, and he had been looking forward to relaxing in his library with a glass of brandy and a good book. Moreover, it was starting to drizzle. 'For heaven's sake get up!'

he said. 'What are you doing here, anyway? I should have thought a woman of your sort would feel more at home in the Haymarket rather than on my doorstep.'

The woman finally looked up at him, displaying her features clearly for the first time. If she heard Lord Rutherford's gasp of surprise, she paid no attention to it.

'What do you mean, *what am I doing here*?' She repeated his question in a tone of voice that suggested she was addressing a mental incompetent. 'I am waiting for my head to explode, of course. It ish . . . it is likely to explode at any minute, you know. My brain has eshpan . . . espant . . . epshan . . . Oh *fiddle*! My brain has grown bigger and it no longer fits inside my skull.'

She touched her hand briefly to her forehead, as if to make certain of the truth of her statement. She then untied the tattered ribbons of her bonnet and pulled it off with a quick, impatient toss of her head. A glorious mass of dark chestnut curls spilled out over her shoulders. 'You see?' she said. 'My hat is now too small for my head, although yesterday it fitted perfectly. Not that it matters, for it's a tatty old bonnet anyway, and I have always disliked it mosht . . . most particularly.'

The brief spate of loquacity apparently exhausted her, for she leaned back against the railings, closing her eyes to shut out the blue glow of a near-by gas street lamp. Her head drooped on to her chest, and she gave every appearance of settling back to sleep.

Lord Rutherford found himself temporarily deprived of the power of speech. He stared at the woman, scarcely able to believe what he saw. She was indescribably beautiful, and the classical purity of her features seemed all the more startling when contrasted with the voluptuous profusion of dark curls that tumbled around her shoulders.

His first coherent thought was that, however much she had drunk, it was amazing that the possessor of such a ravishing face did not seem more prosperous. His gaze flicked over her clothes in quick appraisal, confirming his impression that they were dowdy and virtually worn out. Not at all what he'd have expected to find on a woman of such incredible, sensuous beauty. He looked at her again, wondering if she was setting him up for some elaborate swindle, but he decided she wasn't faking sleep. She remained collapsed against the railings, her shoulders resting against the iron bars, and her eyes tightly closed.

Lord Rutherford gave a testy shrug of his shoulders. The only sensible course was to walk away and leave her to her fate. He reached the bottom step of the marble staircase leading up to his front door before he turned abruptly. Impelled by an irresistible urge he didn't attempt to justify, he marched back to the crouching figure. He bent down and clasped her chin, jerking her head round so that she would open her eyes and he could look at her again. He took considerable care not to get too close to the appalling smell wafting up from her clothes. Not only gin, but fish and vinegar as well, he thought wryly.

His fingers tightened round her chin and she

opened her eyes. They were a startling azure blue. He was silent for a very long time.

'You are drunk,' he said at last.

The azure of her eyes darkened to indigo. 'You are impershinent, sir.'

'Impertinent I may be, but you, my dear, are more than merely drunk. You are entirely cast away.'

For a few seconds she looked at him angrily, without replying. Then she closed her eyes again, as if even the pale glow of the gas light was too strong for her to tolerate. 'I had four daffies of gin and three eel pies,' she said. 'Nashurly . . . nacherly . . . *naturally*, I am drunk, although it is very rude of you to mention it. And you shouldn't say cast away to a lady. That is slang, and most indelicate. You should say intoshi . . . intosicash . . .' She gave up the hopeless struggle to enunciate more clearly. 'You shouldn't pass personal remarks about a lady,' she concluded reprovingly.

'Ladies don't get drunk,' he said.

She sighed, opening her eyes very wide. 'How true!' she exclaimed mournfully. Her expression suddenly lightened, and she looked at him with a dazzling smile. 'I am not sure if I can recommend the gin, but have you any idea how good eel pies actually taste?'

'No,' he replied dryly. 'Eel pies are a pleasure that has so far been denied me.'

'If you would care to try one, I can recommend Jack's Pie Stall on the southern end of Battersea Bridge.'

'I shall bear your hearty recommendation in

mind. What is your name, young woman, and where do you live? Don't you realise that it's dangerous for a woman to go about unescorted at this hour of night?'

A brief shadow touched the brilliance of her eyes, but it was quickly banished. 'I am Mary Smith,' she said.

He noticed that she answered only one of his questions, and he was sure even that answer was a lie, but he simply shrugged to indicate his indifference. There was no reason to expect the girl to tell him the truth and he had no real interest in discovering her name. In fact, he had no legitimate reason to pursue his questions, and common sense suggested he should leave the girl exactly as he had found her. The rain was descending with increasing force and his light evening cape was already drenched. It was ridiculous that he, John, Lord Rutherford, should be kneeling on the pavement, conducting a conversation with some drunken woman of the streets. He deliberately smothered the last embers of his curiosity and got to his feet. The woman held on grimly to the railings and dragged herself up with him.

This time she had no difficulty in remaining standing. They looked at one another in a strange, speculative silence, and it was Lord Rutherford who looked away first. He bent down and picked up the bonnet she had discarded earlier, shaking off as much of the mud as he could. He held it out to her and, when she made no move to take it, placed it firmly on her head, smoothing the damp curls off her forehead and tucking them under the soggy brim of the hat. It was odd, he thought, how clean and sweet-smelling her hair seemed.

He was annoyed at this evidence of his continuing awareness of a girl who should mean nothing at all to him. 'It is time you went home,' he said curtly, avoiding her eyes. 'I have already warned you that the police are likely to pick you up if you loiter here any longer.'

'Yes, sir.' She said nothing more, but he received the distinct impression that she was no longer as drunk as she had been only a few seconds earlier. Something had caused her to sober up in a hurry. He turned his back on her, suddenly unable to tolerate the misery he read in the blue depths of her gaze. 'Get to some lodgings, girl,' he said, and pulled a golden guinea from his waistcoat pocket, thrusting it into her unresponsive hand. He walked away quickly without looking back.

He was turning his key in the front-door lock—only his valet was required to wait up for him after midnight—when he felt a tiny, cold hand touch his wrist. He hesitated in the act of opening the door.

'What do you want?' he asked, his gaze fixed firmly upon the lock.

'I have nowhere to go. Could you . . . would you . . . allow me to sleep somewhere in your house?'

'In my bed, perhaps?' Lord Rutherford did not attempt to conceal his sneer as he turned round to face the girl. His gaze raked her insultingly, while he cursed himself for a fool. He had been wasting his pity. As far as he could judge, the girl was now stone-cold sober. She was obviously a prostitute, and a second-rate drunken one at that. Only a veteran drinker would be able to shake off the effects of alcohol with such amazing rapidity. Only a veteran harlot would proposition him with such boldness.

'I'm afraid you've misjudged your market,' he said, and his expression hardened into coldness. 'I am fastidious about the women I take into my bed. You are half-drunk, unwashed and your choice of perfume utterly fails to excite me. Boiled whelk, is it not, with a generous dash of malt vinegar?'

'I expect it is the eel pies,' she said. 'You remember, I already told you about the eel pies.' For a fleeting moment he could have sworn she looked stricken by his words, but she had her voice well under control, and it sounded soft and faintly husky. Her lashes dropped quickly over her eyes and she turned away without saying anything more.

Lord Rutherford uttered a lengthy stream of profanity. He reflected with a touch of self-mockery that it seemed to be his night for mumbling curses. His voice was harsh when he spoke to the girl. 'I gave you some money,' he said. 'Use it.'

She looked down at her clenched fist and slowly opened it. She stared at the dull gleam of the golden coin as if seeing it for the first time. 'I didn't realise what you had given me,' she said. 'Thank you. I am sorry to have troubled you.'

She walked down the steps, her back ramrod straight. Only the tight, almost convulsive, clutch of her hand on the railing indicated that she was having some difficulty in maintaining her appearance of sober dignity.

'Wait! Come back here, girl!'

She half-turned at the sound of his harsh command but she did not come back. 'Where are you going?' he asked. 'Where do you expect to find a bed at this time of night?'

Her face was in profile, shadowed by the dowdy bonnet, and he could see nothing of her expression. 'I am going to the Haymarket, sir. I am sure I shall find a landlady there whose choice in perfumes is less discriminating than your own.'

He discovered that he was listening almost obsessively to the attractive lilt of her voice, and his brain began to seethe with an outrageous idea. It might work, he thought, and it would certainly solve some crushing problems in his immediate future. After all, she sounded like a lady, and her looks were stunning. He suddenly realised the full absurdity of what he was thinking, and thrust the idea out of his mind, not daring to explore it any further. She was a woman of the streets, for heaven's sake! God knew what she would look like in the fresh light of morning, when she had sobered up and he had returned to his senses.

But was there any harm in giving her a bed, so that he could review his reckless scheme in the morning? He, after all, had little to lose by such an action and the woman would gain a free bed for the night. He spoke to her abruptly, still half-convinced that he was behaving like a fool. He avoided looking at her perfect profile which distracted him so much and revealed so little of what she was thinking. 'I could find you a bed in my servants' quarters, if you would like me to do so,' he said.

'Oh, would you really? I should be so grateful
. . . you cannot imagine what it would mean to
me . . .' The face which the girl turned to him was
radiant with new happiness.

Lord Rutherford frowned as he pushed open his
front door. 'Do not imagine you will be free to
roam around and make off with the family silver. I
have every intention of locking you in whichever
room I give you.'

'I am not a thief.' The azure eyes met his gaze
defiantly.

Lord Rutherford smiled cynically. 'I am sure you
are not,' he said. 'At least some of the time.' He
conducted her quickly through his cavernous entrance hall, giving her no chance to reply. For some
reason he found her conversation curiously un-
settling. 'The servants' quarters are through here,'
he said, indicating a heavily-panelled, white-
painted door. 'Will you follow me?'

He watched to make sure that she followed him
along the narrow uncarpeted corridor, and finally
halted in the doorway of a tiny room located at the
very back of the house. The room was not more
than eight feet wide and the outer wall ran with
damp. It was this damp which had caused the
boot-boy to be evacuated to a more comfortable
corner in one of the attics. There was no furniture
in the room save for an iron bed-frame, strung with
rope. The straw pallet, normally used as a mattress,
had been removed to prevent mildew.

'Your room,' Lord Rutherford said brusquely.

'Thank you. It is very good of you to provide me
with shelter.'

There was no mistaking the sincerity of the girl's gratitude, and Lord Rutherford swallowed a small exclamation of annoyance. He had no obligation to make elaborate provisions for the girl's comfort. The room, he assured himself, was a great deal dryer and cleaner than the pavement, and the spartan bed-frame could be padded by folding her cloak. Perversely, her polite acceptance of the dreary accommodation infuriated him, tugging at his conscience. He looked angrily at the girl. 'I shall return in a minute,' he said.

He slammed the unpainted wooden door, locking her in with a sharp turn of the rusty iron key. She might as well be spending the night in gaol, he reflected, as in that dreary hole. He pushed the thought away and marched down the corridor, his dark brows contracted in a frown. Damn it, he was not going to allow himself to feel guilty. A beautiful face and azure blue eyes were not going to lull him into giving some trollop from the streets the run of his house. He wrenched open the door leading to the kitchens. Where the hell did the housekeeper store his bedclothes?

He pulled open a few doors without finding a single piece of linen. He possessed, it seemed, fourteen cupboards full of china and a dozen full of preserved fruits and marmalade, but the downstairs cupboards didn't contain even a table-napkin, let alone a bed-sheet. Thoroughly out of humour with himself and the world, Lord Rutherford stormed upstairs to the nearest guest-room, where he pulled a pillow and two blankets off the bed and marched downstairs again.

The girl was standing just where he had left her, but her hands were clasped around her body as if she were very cold, and she seemed unnaturally still. Lord Rutherford stepped only a few paces inside the doorway.

'Here! Make use of these if you wish.' He tossed the blankets and pillow on to the iron bedstead. 'I'll see you in the morning,' he said curtly. 'Goodnight.'

'Goodnight, sir.' As he closed the door he saw that she took two shaky steps before collapsing on to the makeshift bed. Her sins of over-indulgence catching up on her, no doubt, he thought cynically. He could have saved himself the trouble of ransacking the house looking for blankets. She hadn't even bothered to remove her boots, much less ask for water to wash her face and hands before falling into bed. Lord Rutherford cursed himself. He was an utter fool to have brought her inside the house. Of course he couldn't possibly go ahead with his plan. It was only the accumulated frustrations of a difficult evening that had put such a ridiculous notion into his head. He paused for a moment outside his library door, but somehow the thought of drinking a solitary glass of cognac was no longer appealing. Even the prospect of re-reading Sir Walter Scott's *Rob Roy* could not tempt him into the library.

With a sigh compounded equally of weariness and frustration, he climbed the marble staircase to his rooms. He flung off his sodden cape and rang for his valet. He felt dishevelled, as if he needed a great deal of soap and hot water to clean himself, and the smell of stale eel pie lingered on his nostrils.

He removed his golden cufflinks while he waited for the valet to arrive, dropping them absent-mindedly on his huge mahogany dressing-table. He would get rid of the girl first thing tomorrow, he decided. He would arrange for her to be given breakfast and then he personally would escort her from the premises. He was sure that when he saw her in the harsh light of morning he would no longer find her so damnably attractive. Powder and paint that looked wonderful under the glow of a gas-lamp would look a great deal less appealing in the bright light of day.

He nodded an abstracted greeting as his valet came into the room.

'Good evening, my lord,' the servant said, bowing politely.

'Sorry to disturb you at such a late hour, Griggs. I should like some hot water, please.'

'Yes, my lord. I have kept a kettle boiling on the stove. Wonderfully convenient those new kitchen ranges are. A few lumps of coal and they'll keep going all night.'

'I'm pleased that you find them practical.' Lord Rutherford smothered a yawn as the valet left the room in pursuit of hot water. He shrugged off his tightly-fitting evening coat and sank into an armchair drawn up close to the fire. God, but he was tired. He closed his eyes, shutting out the dancing images of the firelight, and immediately he could visualise the girl's perfect features as clearly as though she were standing in front of him. What a pity she was a drunkard, he thought as he slid away into sleep, because she was undoubtedly the most beautiful woman he had ever seen.

CHAPTER
THREE

THE REPEATED banging at the door reverberated inside Deborah's head, each rap like a sharp blow from a hammer. She groaned, then turned groggily, burying her face in the pillow. It was no use. The peremptory knocking continued, driving away the last blissful remnants of sleep.

As soon as she was fully awake, she realised that she was dying. She knew beyond any possibility of doubt that no human being could feel as wretched as she and expect to survive for more than an hour or so. She pulled the blankets over her head, frowning irritably when the banging continued. She had no intention of getting out of bed when she could die with so much less discomfort lying down.

'Go away!' she croaked. She licked her dry lips and tried to repeat her command more forcefully, but her parched throat produced only an incomprehensible squawking. She squeaked a few times, then gave up the struggle and concentrated her attention on feeling miserable. She wondered whether she would die of the ache in her head before the pain in her stomach carried her off, or vice versa.

She was still pondering this problem when she

felt a hand grab her by the shoulders and start to shake her vigorously. She clenched her teeth to prevent nausea overwhelming her, and reluctantly sat upright in the narrow bed.

She immediately wished that she hadn't moved. A dazzling array of rockets exploded behind her eyeballs, and her stomach heaved with a fresh spasm of sickness. With a great effort of will she managed to raise first one eyelid, then the other. After a while, the rockets stopped exploding and she found herself staring at a formidable expanse of black bombasine. Mrs Pritchard's bosom, she thought wretchedly, and dragged her gaze upward.

But it was not her landlady's sour face that greeted her. Despite the similarity of black-draped mounds of flesh, this woman was younger than Mrs Pritchard, although she looked no more friendly. Her mouth was drawn into a thin line, and her nose was wrinkled with distaste. Deborah could sympathise with the woman's pinched nostrils. The room where she found herself was permeated by a strong odour of stale fish.

'So, you're finally awake,' the woman said. 'You'd better get up and make haste about it, Lord Rutherford wishes to see you.' Her tone of voice suggested that Lord Rutherford's wishes were not to be questioned, but that they were, in this instance, quite incomprehensible.

Deborah held one hand to her forehead and the other to her stomach. 'Who is Lord Rutherford?' she asked.

The woman's lips snapped so tightly together that they seemed to disappear. 'I should think you

would know Lord Rutherford is the master here,'
she said. 'And I am Mrs Bowler, Lord Rutherford's
housekeeper.'

'Oh.' Deborah experimentally released her grip
on her stomach and found that her insides remained more or less in place. She pressed both
hands to her forehead in an effort to think. Lord
Rutherford! She was quite sure she had never
heard the name before. Who on earth was he? And
what was she doing in his house?

She was not given any more time to straighten
out her thoughts. 'You have to get up at once,' the
housekeeper said. 'Come along now, stir yourself,
if you please. You'll need to wash before you see
his lordship, and you've already kept him waiting
for the best part of thirty minutes.'

The prospect of a wash was most appealing.
Deborah obediently clutched the sides of the bed
and swung her feet to the ground, doing her best to
ignore the strange rippling movement of the walls.
She searched round for her shoes, and discovered
to her chagrin that she was wearing them. Gingerly
she pulled herself upright and, with considerable
caution, let go of the iron bed-frame. She was
relieved to discover that she could stand without its
support.

Mrs Bowler cast one look at Deborah's wild,
unkempt hair, then allowed her gaze to travel
slowly over her muddy, fish-stained garments and
dust-streaked hands. She said nothing, but her face
hardened into lines of the utmost disapproval and
she turned abruptly away. 'Follow me,' she said
curtly.

Deborah did her best to obey the command, although she was forced to clutch at the wall a couple of times as the housekeeper marched down a long, whitewashed corridor. They stopped outside a small bathroom, dimly lit by a narrow skylight. 'You may wash here,' Mrs Bowler said. 'I shall wait for you.'

'Thank you.' Deborah leaned against the cast-iron sink as cold water trickled into it from the solitary tap. She was suddenly seized by a raging thirst, and she cupped her hands to capture the flow, sucking greedily at the cool water, feeling it soothe the dryness of her throat. The hammering inside her skull gradually muted itself to a dull ache, and she began to consider the possibility that she might live to see another night.

When her thirst was finally sated, she washed in the cold water, rinsing her face repeatedly and scrubbing her hands and arms with a bar of carbolic soap she found on the side of the sink. There was no brush or comb in the little bathroom, and most of her hairpins were lost, but she braided her hair as best she could, pinning it back as tightly as her few pins would allow. There was no mirror in the room and, glancing down at her rumpled clothes, Deborah decided that was just as well.

She took another drink of cold water, and the churning in her stomach finally ceased. The brisk wash seemed to have cleared her mind of much of its haziness, but she was far from grateful for the sudden clarity of her memories. How did one greet a nobleman, she wondered, who had first seen one lying in a drunken stupor on the pavement outside

his house? *Good morning, Lord Rutherford. I'm
most frightfully sorry for selecting your front doorstep to collapse on.* All things considered, such a
remark hardly seemed adequate to the demands of
the occasion.

She controlled a faintly hysterical gasp of laughter and opened the bathroom door. She was
greeted by the sight of Mrs Bowler's folded arms
and disapproving features. Deborah's hands began
to shake, so she clasped them tightly together,
hiding them in the folds of her shabby gown. She
drew in a deep breath and compelled herself to
meet the housekeeper's gaze. 'I am ready for you to
take me to Lord Rutherford,' she said.

The housekeeper did not deign to reply. She
walked off, bosom heaving, and Deborah shuffled
along in her wake. Her momentary bravado had
entirely deserted her. Whatever Lord Rutherford
wanted to say, she knew it could not possibly be
pleasant.

They halted outside a brightly polished mahogany door, and the housekeeper tapped three
times on the gleaming panels.

'Yes?'

'The young person you wished to see is waiting in
the hall, my lord.'

'Send her in, please, Mrs Bowler, and then you
may leave us.'

Deborah responded to the housekeeper's nod
and walked into the warm, book-filled study. She
felt acutely embarrassed by every aspect of her
encounter with Lord Rutherford, but she was determined to thank him with all the sincerity and

formal courtesy she could muster. Some small remnant of personal dignity might yet be rescued if he
should prove to be a sympathetic listener. The door
closed softly behind her. She looked up to greet her
rescuer, and the polite words of gratitude died
away, unspoken.

Lord Rutherford was seated at a desk in front of
a large, mullioned window. The morning sun
flooded the room, catching his dark hair in a halo of
brightness while at the same time casting his face
into shadow. As Deborah entered the room, he
stood up and scrutinised her with silent and un-
nerving thoroughness. In the harsh contrast of
light, the set of his features appeared aloof,
touched with arrogance, and his mouth seemed so
rigidly controlled that Deborah wondered if he had
ever in his entire life allowed himself to express a
spontaneous emotion.

He walked over to the hearth, and stood in front
of the blazing fire. He rested one booted foot on the
brass fender, but neither his body nor his manner contained the slightest hint of relaxation.
'Good morning,' he said. 'I hope that you slept
well?'

If anything, his voice was cooler, more remote,
than his expression, and Deborah felt a flush of
colour wash her cheeks as he continued his de-
tached inspection of her appearance. She was dis-
concertingly conscious of the mud-spattered hem
of her gown and the wisps of loose hair curling
round her neck and cheeks, but when she replied
she did her best to match his own dispassionate
courtesy. 'Yes, thank you, my lord. I slept well and

I am grateful to you for providing me with shelter for the night.'

He inclined his head in barest acknowledgment of her thanks. 'I trust you have also recovered from your—indisposition—of yesterday evening?' He reached into the pocket of his waistcoat, and withdrew a heavy gold pocket-watch. Flipping it open, he glanced down at its face, smothering a discreet yawn. Every line of his body spoke of indifference to her reply.

She was suddenly annoyed by the completeness of his self-possession, the tacit mockery of his question. 'I wasn't indisposed,' she said curtly. 'I was drunk. Hopelessly, totally drunk.'

For a fraction of a second his body was utterly still, then he closed the watch with a sudden sharp snap and slipped it back into his pocket. When he looked at Deborah again, his face was as cold as before, and she realised she must have imagined the fleeting moment of amusement she had glimpsed in his eyes.

'What is your name?' he asked brusquely.

'Mary Brown.'

'Last night it was Mary Smith,' he said. 'Is your brain so pickled in gin that you no longer remember your own name?'

'Does it matter?' she asked. 'My lord, I am deeply grateful to you for the kindness you showed me last night, but I should not disturb you any longer. I must be on my way.'

'Where are you going? What are you planning to do?'

She wished that her hands would stop trembling.

She wished that she knew the answer to his question. She wished that she wasn't so very frightened. 'I don't know exactly,' she said. 'I must look for work.'

'And what, precisely, is your line of work?'

'I hope to find work as a shop assistant, or I thought I might apply for a job as a nursemaid. I am very fond of young children . . .' Her voice died away beneath the unconcealed irony of his gaze.

'I would have thought there were other positions for which you were better qualified,' he said, and this time he made no attempt to conceal his mockery. 'You must be aware of the fact that your personal attractions are quite startling. Your face and figure both seem nearly perfect, in so far as one can judge underneath that bundle of rags you are wearing. I would have thought you ideally suited to a career in the theatre. I cannot believe you have never considered making practical use of your— feminine attributes.'

She knew that for some reason he was deliberately setting out to insult her, but she controlled her anger without too much difficulty. The past few months had taught her invaluable lessons in self-control. 'If you have visited a playhouse recently, my lord, you must be aware of the fact that a stage career requires more than a pretty face. It is necessary to have boundless energy and considerable talent as an actress, a singer or a dancer.'

He raised one eyebrow in supercilious disbelief. 'You evidently have more—intimate—knowledge of the requirements than I. My experience would suggest that you are exaggerating the demands of the profession. There are innumerable young women who claim to be actresses and who possess none of the talents you have mentioned. One assumes, of course, that their income is not derived entirely from their performance in front of the footlights.'

For a moment, her anger threatened to burst out of the restraints she had put upon it. She hated him in that moment for his calm assumption of moral superiority, and for his praise of her beauty that was in reality no more than a cover for his insults. She didn't speak until her feelings were once again under complete control. 'I am grateful for your advice, Lord Rutherford, I shall bear it in mind when I am looking for work. If I have not yet thanked you sufficiently for the shelter you provided last night, please allow me to do so now.'

'No thanks are necessary.'

'Then, with your permission, I should like to be on my way. I must find work before nightfall.'

'I would like to talk to you for a little longer,' he said. 'I shall order breakfast in a while. Do you not wish to eat before you leave? I could ask the cook to prepare some eggs and sausages, and perhaps a slice or two of smoked ham . . .'

She was aware of the bribe implicit in his words and was tempted to spurn his tantalising promise of food. She had been unable to afford the price of breakfast for so long that she had lost the habit of eating in the morning. Moreover, her stomach was still queasy with the after-effects of too much gin. Anger and pride both tempted her to march out of the room, but common sense, a commodity she had recently found far more useful than pride, intervened. If she ate a hearty breakfast she wouldn't need to buy any food for the rest of the day. In her present circumstances, she was quite willing to trade a few minutes of her time in exchange for a nourishing, well-cooked meal.

'It is so generous of you to offer me breakfast,' she said, forcing the words out to the accompaniment of a stiff smile. 'I am sure I have done nothing to merit such a favour.'

She saw the line of his jaw tighten as he registered the underlying sarcasm of her reply. He looked up sharply. 'Precisely why did you get drunk last night?' he asked.

His question caught her momentarily off guard, but she was too wary to be betrayed into total honesty. 'I drank gin on an empty stomach and I am not used to consuming spirituous liquor in any form. I am not in the habit of getting drunk, my lord. In fact, it has never happened before.' As soon as she had spoken, she wondered why she had told him even that much of the truth. It would surely have been better to let him imagine she was well-used to the joys of the gin bottle. She didn't want him to start enquiring too closely into her background.

'What happened last night to precipitate your sudden acquaintance with the demon drink?' The faintest of smiles touched the hardness of his mouth. 'Could you not trust me with the truth, Mary? I promise that if you are in trouble I shall do my best to help you.'

To her surprise, she had to fight an almost irresistible urge to confide in him. His manner was so
authoritative that it was tempting simply to answer
with complete honesty. Perhaps, if he knew the
whole truth, he would be prepared to help her find
a job. Deborah quickly dismissed the dangerous
thought. The past few months had taught her that it
was safest to rely only on herself. She had already
learned the first and most important lesson of the
disadvantaged: the less people knew about you, the
less they could hurt you. She was determined not to
forget a lesson learned with so much pain. She
stared into the blazing coals, watching the bright
scarlet and yellow glow as the flames roared up the
chimney. She didn't look at him when she finally
spoke. 'There was no particular reason, my lord. I
just felt in the mood for a bit of fun.'

'So for no particular reason—at least that you are
prepared to reveal to me—you decided last night to
go and make yourself roaring drunk. Do you plan
to follow the same schedule of entertainment
tonight?'

She made a small, involuntary movement of
protest, then quickly quelled her instinctive words
of denial. There was no good reason to correct his
false impression of her, and many good reasons for
remaining silent. 'It is kind of you to trouble yourself about me, my lord, but I don't think my plans
for the future can be of any interest to a great
nobleman such as yourself.'

'Suffice it to say that they are.' He looked at her,
and this time there was no mistaking the hint of
laughter lurking in his gaze. 'As a great nobleman, I

am permitted the occasional idiosyncrasy, you know.'

She would not let herself respond to his laughter. Perhaps, after all, she had imagined it. 'My lord, it is already nearly ten o'clock. I have to leave here . . . I *must* find work . . .'

'Where are your parents?' he asked abruptly. 'Can neither of them help you to obtain a decent job?'

'My parents are both dead, my lord. My father had a private . . . my father did not pursue any particular career and my mother was an opera singer. Unfortunately, I lacked the talent to follow in her footsteps.'

'An opera singer!' Lord Rutherford murmured, almost to himself. 'I was not so far wrong in my guess, after all.' He swung round. 'Did your mother try to train you as a—singer?'

Deborah paid no attention to the subtle hesitation of his question. She could not restrain a fond, reminiscent smile as she remembered her music lessons. She had been almost nine when her mother finally accepted the sad fact that her only child possessed a singing voice more closely related to the cawing of a crow than the trilling of an angel. She glanced up, the smile still lingering in her eyes. 'Whatever you may think to the contrary, my lord, opera singers today are required to do more than wear gaudy clothes and hum a tuneful melody. They are required to sing with power and beauty and great technical skill. I am not qualified to become a singer for the simple reason that I lack the essential requirement of a beautiful voice.'

'I see. But what of your other relatives? If your parents are dead, surely there must be somebody who could care for you?'

'Nobody, my lord.' She spoke with absolute finality. She had no intention of expanding on the subject of Cousin George and his cloth mills, neither did she wish to explain that her mother's family had utterly repudiated their daughter when she married an English Protestant of modest means.

Lord Rutherford spoke into the fire. 'Your situation is almost without hope, is it not? Your prospects for the future look somewhat grim.'

'I would not . . . I wouldn't say that, my lord. I dare say I shall find a job soon.'

'As a kitchen-maid?' he said shortly. 'Or on the streets, which is where we both know you are most likely to end up?' He fell silent, and Deborah became aware of an increasing tension in the atmosphere of the room. Moisture escaped from one of the lumps of coal, piercing the silence with a long, low hiss. Lord Rutherford used the tongs to add another lump of coal from the scuttle, then walked to the window and stared out into the garden. As far as Deborah could judge, he was lost in contemplation of a horse-chestnut tree. She wondered if she should take this opportunity to slip out of the room. To all appearances, he had completely forgotten her presence.

He turned abruptly, putting paid to her tentative thoughts of escape. 'It is conceivable that I might be able to offer you employment,' he said. 'I have not yet entirely made up my mind.'

'You might have a job for me?' she whispered. She felt her legs begin to buckle under her and tears of relief welled up, refusing to be held in check. She scrubbed furiously at the wetness with the back of her hand, wishing she still owned a handkerchief. During all the weeks she had been searching for work she had held her emotions rigidly in check, never once allowing herself to cry. It was only when Lord Rutherford mentioned the possibility of a job that she realised how great a burden of fear she had been carrying. The unexpected hope of employment was so overwhelming that she was afraid she might faint. She walked shakily across the room and clutched the edge of Lord Rutherford's desk.

'You have a job for me?' she repeated, unable to keep the desperate eagerness from her voice. 'You could provide me with employment? I would be willing to do anything. No task would be too menial, I assure you.'

He addressed her from the window. 'I said only that it is possible. I have promised nothing as yet.' His voice was harsh and his gaze flicked angrily over her flushed cheeks and tear-bright eyes. His mouth tightened as he handed her his handkerchief. 'Here, use this,' he said. He walked across to the fireplace and tugged on the bell-rope. A footman appeared almost at once. 'We wish for some tea,' Lord Rutherford said curtly. 'And some buttered toast.'

He gestured to a chair as soon as the footman left. 'Sit down,' he said, 'and perhaps we may start again. What is your name? And this time, I would appreciate the truth, if you please.'

Her hesitation lasted no more than a second. 'I am Deborah Phipps.'

'I shall ask you once more, Miss Phipps, and I beg you to consider your answer carefully. Do you have any family who could help you? Is there no connection of your mother's or your father's who could be persuaded to help you? If you have relatives living outside London, I would be willing to provide you with the train fare to their home.'

'You are very kind,' she said, and this time there was no trace of sarcasm in her words. 'But there is nobody. I am free to take any job you care to offer me, my lord.'

A tap at the door heralded the arrival of a servant pushing a tea-trolley, laden with a silver tea-service and plates of buttered toast and scones. A lighted spirit-lamp kept a kettle of hot water bubbling, promising second helpings of fragrant tea. From the trolley in the centre of the room the wonderful smell of hot bread wafted under Deborah's nose. She suddenly realised that, despite the after-effects of the gin and her shrunken appetite, she was ravenously hungry. She did her best not to look at the enticing piles of food. It required a phenomenal amount of self-control to refrain from seizing a handful of toast and gobbling it down.

'Thank you,' Lord Rutherford said to the servant. 'There is no need for you to wait. We shall serve ourselves.'

The servant was well trained. If he was surprised to find his master taking tea with a woman dressed virtually in rags, he managed to conceal his feelings. He inclined his head in a deferential nod and went out, closing the door quietly behind him. Lord Rutherford turned to Deborah. 'Would you pour for us, Miss Phipps?'

'Certainly, my lord.' She poured tea into one of the delicate china cups, relieved to find that her hand was quite steady. 'Do you take milk or sugar, my lord?'

'A little milk,' he said.

She handed him the cup. 'Would you care for some toast? Or a scone?'

'I will have a scone, thank you.'

She waited until he was seated in a chair by the fire before pouring a cup of tea for herself. He had not invited her to return to her chair, so she remained standing by the tea-trolley. She had to clench her teeth against the side of the cup to prevent herself from gulping the hot tea in one quick parched swallow.

'There is no need to drink standing up, Miss Phipps. Come and sit by the fire. I will draw the trolley closer to the hearth so that we can help ourselves to a second cup without having to get up.'

She sat down stiffly in the armchair opposite his. She sipped slowly at her tea, wondering if she had ever before tasted anything quite as good. As soon as she put down her cup and saucer, Lord Rutherford handed her a plate piled high with toast and scones. 'Here,' he said. 'You will enjoy these. My cook is noted for her light hand.'

His gaze happened to meet her own, and she felt an unexpected surge of gratitude for his thoughtfulness. She smiled at him with all the natural warmth of her nature.

'This tea is so delicious. Thank you, my lord.'

There was a distinct rattle as he replaced his cup on the trolley. 'I have a proposition to put to you, Miss Phipps,' he said. He stood up, flicking a crumb from his immaculate morning suit. 'I own a small cottage in Gloucestershire, which I have been planning to visit for some time. The cottage and surrounding lands are in urgent need of attention. I have decided to leave after luncheon today, and I would like you to come with me.'

She was filled with such happiness that it was almost impossible to speak. 'You need a housekeeper for the cottage?' she asked, hardly daring to put the hope into words. 'Lord Rutherford, I shall work so hard . . . I shall be honoured . . .'

'No,' he said curtly. 'I am not offering you the position of housekeeper. I already have a housekeeper and full complement of servants in residence at the cottage. I merely require your . . . company.'

'Company?' she said, and after a pause added, 'Oh, I see.' She tried to ignore the sickening lump of despair that returned to her throat, choking off her brief moment of happiness. After all this, she was still going to be faced with the terrible dilemma of selling her body or starving to death. The disappointment was all the more fierce because she had been foolish enough to allow herself to hope. 'I suppose you mean that you want me to become . . .' She swallowed hard, struggling to conceal her despair. 'Do you wish me to become your mistress?'

Her question seemed to make him angry. 'I can

imagine few things that I desire less,' he said harshly. 'You have somehow acquired a very inflated sense of your own worth upon the market. In selecting a mistress I require more than a pretty face and a bundle of dirty clothes. You should stroll around Covent Garden one day and inspect your competitors. Believe me, you scarcely measure up.'

'I am sorry if I have been presumptuous,' she said tightly. 'Since I am not qualified to become your mistress, and since you already have all the domestic staff you need, perhaps you would be good enough to explain exactly what you wish me to do?'

'You have merely to accompany me to Gloucestershire and remain there as long as I desire to keep you with me. I dare say you will find odd jobs to do about the house and garden. In view of the circumstances in which I found you, and in view of your non-existent prospects for improvement, I fail to see why you are hesitating. I am offering you a roof over your head and three square meals a day, which is undoubtedly more than you've enjoyed for some considerable time past. In addition, I am prepared to pay you a pound for every week that you remain with me.'

'A pound a week! Fifty pounds a year! And my keep!' Deborah's voice became squeaky with delight. It was a long time since she had allowed herself to dream of earning so much money.

'Don't go into raptures too soon,' Lord Rutherford remarked. 'It is highly unlikely that the job will last for more than a week or two. I doubt if I shall be able to tolerate your company for as long as a month, let alone for an entire year. However, when I dismiss you, I promise to reward you with a bonus of five pounds and your train fare back to London. I shall pay that bonus even if I dismiss you after only a day or two of employment, so you can see that you have everything to gain and nothing to lose by accepting.'

She couldn't afford the luxury of examining his wonderful offer too closely, but some instinct of self-preservation forced her to show a little caution. After all, there was no point in eating heartily tonight only to find herself in deadly peril on the morrow. Despite his austere appearance, he could be a cunning lunatic in one of his lucid moments, for all she knew to the contrary. 'You are sure there will be other servants at this cottage? We shall not be entirely alone?'

'We shall not be alone,' he said. 'Have no fear, I am not planning to lure you to some terrible doom. The cottage is a perfectly normal country residence and there are five or six servants living on the premises. If you do not believe me, you may check the truth of that statement with the housekeeper here. Even you must be able to see at a glance that Mrs Bowler is not a woman to trifle with the truth. Indeed, I am sure you have already observed that Mrs Bowler is not a woman to trifle with anything.'

She wondered if she was again imagining the thread of laughter in his voice. She dismissed the thought as unimportant. Lord Rutherford's sense of humour was of no relevance to her life, but the terms of her employment were crucial. Although two months earlier she would have accepted the job without any attempt at further bargaining, recent experiences had taught her better. This job was not going to last long, and she would soon be job-hunting once again. With respectable clothing and five pounds in her pocket, she would be equipped to apply for a job as a housekeeper or nursemaid. Her first requirement, therefore, was to expand her wardrobe. She smiled at Lord Rutherford with as much charm as she could muster.

'I accept your kind offer, my lord, but I cannot travel with you dressed as I am,' she said. 'Since I am to be in your employment, I am sure you will agree that I need some new clothes before we leave London.'

He scarcely bothered to glance at her. He certainly seemed to pay no attention to her dazzling smile. 'I suppose it would be preferable to travel with someone who is decently clad,' he said.

She scarcely registered the insult, since she had far more practical problems to worry about. 'Do you think you could authorise the purchase of two new outfits, my lord?' She hurried on, not giving him time to refuse. 'In that way, one set of clothes could be laundered while I am wearing the other and you would never have to worry about fish-smells again.'

He tugged at the bell-rope. 'I dare say that is reasonable,' he said indifferently. The footman came into the study and Lord Rutherford's manner, never particularly warm, lost the last traces of emotion. 'I plan to travel on the afternoon train to Cheltenham,' he said to him. 'Miss Phipps wishes to take a bath before we go.'

'Yes, my lord.' This time, the footman's training did not quite prevent his curiosity from showing. He slipped a quick, disbelieving glance in Deborah's direction. 'The young woman . . . er . . . the young lady is going with you, my lord?'

'Yes.' Lord Rutherford apparently saw no need to enlarge upon his reply. 'Please tell Mrs Bowler that I wish to speak with her immediately.'

The footman bowed. 'I will see about the hot water for the young lady's bath, my lord. Would you come with me, please, miss?'

Lord Rutherford pulled out his pocket-watch. 'Don't be too long,' he said to Deborah. 'I don't want to miss the train. The housekeeper will bring your new clothes to you.'

She curtsied. 'Thank you, my lord.' The footman was already in the hall, but Deborah hesitated for a moment in the doorway. 'I am truly grateful for all you have done for me, my lord. I shall try my very best to give you every satisfaction.'

'Will you? Perhaps it would be better for all of us if you do not try too hard.'

The footman coughed. 'Will that be all, my lord?'

Lord Rutherford did not look up. 'Yes,' he said. 'That will be all.'

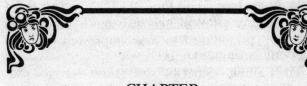

CHAPTER
FOUR

THE FOOTMAN, very much on his dignity, conducted Deborah to the servants' bathroom which, he informed her, was recently renovated and contained the very latest in porcelain bathtubs.

'You may perform your ablutions here, miss,' He said, throwing open the door with a flourish. 'I shall send in a maid with the 'ot water and a towel.'

Deborah looked at the modern bathtub with its shiny brass taps. 'Doesn't the hot water supply work?' she asked.

The footman bristled at this suggestion of criticism. 'The 'ot water geyser works a treat once it's turned on,' he said sharply. 'But it isn't turned on at the moment since we only requires 'ot water on Fridays and Saturdays when the domestic staff of this household 'as their baths. Females is supposed to use this bathroom on a Saturday night.'

Deborah bit back a tiny bubble of laughter. 'I am sorry to have interfered with the household's routine,' she said.

The footman merely sniffed. 'If you wait here, miss, I'll send in the 'ot water immediately. The kitchen boiler works twenty-four hours a day,

seven days a week, and you'll have to admit there
isn't many 'ouseholds as can say that.'

Deborah managed to look impressed. 'Indeed
not,' she murmured politely.

The footman departed and a skivvy arrived moments later, carrying a huge enamel pail and with a
white bathtowel tucked under her arm. Steam
curled out from beneath the lid of the bucket, but
the young maid seemed untroubled by the weight
and heat of her burden. She chattered cheerfully as
she poured out the boiling water. ''Ow are you,
miss?' she said. 'Looking forward to your bath, I
'spect. There's nothing like a 'ot bath, is there? My
Mam can't believe as I'm allowed one every week.'
She set the empty bucket down and pointed to the
brown rubber bathplug as if she expected Deborah
to be unfamiliar with such modern luxuries. 'You
have only to lift that up, miss, when you've finished
washing, and all the water goes down the 'ole.
There's a pipe what leads straight from the bath to
the sewer.' She lowered her voice to indicate her
awe. 'This 'ouse has got pipes running all over it,
even upstairs. Do you know, 'is lordship has *two*
bathrooms on the second floor with 'ot and cold
water going right in! The 'ot water is pumped up
through the walls and then the dirty water runs
back out. Gives you the creeps when you think
about it, dunnit? I mean to say, I've bin 'ere three
years already, and never 'ad to carry a single pail of
dirty water down the stairs.'

She turned on the cold tap and added enough
water to cover the bottom of the bathtub with two
inches of tepid water. She then stood back and

examined her handiwork with evident satisfaction. 'It's wonderful what they can do nowadays to make 'ousework easy.'

Deborah, who had carried her own bathwater for the first time when she arrived at Mrs Pritchard's lodging-house, smiled her agreement. 'Yes, it must make a big difference for you, especially in the kitchen.'

'My Mam says I don't know the meaning of 'ard woik, an' I dare say she's right.' The skivvy grinned cheerfully. I'm sure you'll like working for 'is lordship. He's a good man, even if 'e doesn't never crack a smile. And I 'eard tell that Gloucestershire's a pretty part of the country. Meself, I prefer Lunnon. It's got a bit of life to it, if you know what I mean. Well, I'll leave you to your bath, miss, seeing as 'ow your water's getting cold. Can you find your way back to your room when you're finished? It's only just down the corridor a bit.'

'Yes, I can find my way. Thank you for the hot water.'

'No trouble.' The maid left, and Deborah stepped into the bath. She was amused, and perhaps a little relieved, to discover that in at least one respect Lord Rutherford's household was exactly like any other. He had offered her employment only about twenty minutes previously and already the entire staff, right down to the kitchen-maid, knew that she was accompanying him to his cottage. She scrubbed herself clean, using a great deal of soap and relishing the luxury of warm water, another commodity she had been unable to afford for nearly two weeks. She was reluctant to put on her dirty clothes once she was dry, but she had no choice, and so she slipped into them and hurried back to her tiny room.

She had not been waiting many minutes when Mrs Bowler arrived, accompanied by another maid. They were both loaded with parcels, and Mrs Bowler was flushed and panting.

'I have done as his lordship instructed,' the housekeeper said. 'The master is determined to catch the afternoon train, so I had no time for searching from store to store. You will find those parcels contain two complete new outfits, which is what his lordship told me to buy. There is even a new pair of walking-boots included, and everything is of the same quality as I buy for myself. I selected garments that may be a little on the large side, miss, since it's better to be safe than sorry.'

'I am sure everything will be satisfactory,' Deborah said. 'And if the clothes are too large, I can easily take them in a little. I enjoy sewing.'

The housekeeper looked as if she wished to say something cutting, but could think of nothing appropriate. She compromised by frowning, and pursing her lips even more tightly than before. 'Come, Margaret,' she said to her underling. 'We have a great deal to do if his lordship is to catch the afternoon train. And you, miss, are to join us for luncheon in the servants' hall. We eat at one o'clock as soon as the master has finished his meal.'

'I'll come to the kitchen when I've changed,' Deborah said. She could hardly wait to open the parcels resting on the bed behind her. New clothes!

It seemed a lifetime since she had last had the pleasure of stepping into unpatched underwear. She smiled gratefully at the two servants, ignoring the housekeeper's wrathful expression. Ever since Lord Rutherford offered her a job, it had seemed as if she couldn't stop smiling. 'Thank you, Mrs Bowler, for all that you've done for me. You must have rushed round to buy all these clothes so quickly.'

The housekeeper's frown remained firmly in place. It was all too evident that she was deeply suspicious of a woman who spoke like an aristocrat, had the dazzling beauty of somebody who was no better than she ought to be, but was dressed in rags. 'I am always anxious to please Lord Rutherford,' she said primly. 'Come along, Margaret, stop dilly-dallying.' She walked out, not bothering to close the door, and Deborah heard the maid say, 'She's ever so pretty, isn't she, Mrs Bowler?'

'Just you keep your mind on your duties, Margaret, and remember what you've been told before. Handsome is as handsome does.'

'I only meant that she had a nice smile. Friendly, like.'

A bend in the corridor carried the two servants out of earshot. Deborah turned back to the packages, but some of her pleasure had vanished under the weight of Mrs Bowler's open disapproval. Was she being foolish to accept Lord Rutherford's offer of a job without insisting on knowing more about it? Why should he want her to join him in a country cottage where he already had five or six servants unless . . . Unless what? Did she really think he was planning to seduce her? Expressed so bluntly, the idea seemed absurd.

It was most unfortunate, Deborah thought, that virtuous women had so little idea of how men treated women they were planning to seduce. How could she protect herself from seduction when she wasn't at all sure what the process of seduction actually involved? She knew that allowing one's dance partner to escort one from the ballroom floor to an unlighted veranda was a step towards ruin, but since there was no possibility of finding herself dancing with Lord Rutherford, this rule for self-protection was not as helpful as it might have been.

Deborah shrugged her shoulders with unladylike impatience. Young girls were warned from childhood about the silken inducements to vice that unscrupulous men might hold out to them, and anything less silken than Lord Rutherford's manner would be hard to imagine.

She deliberately shook off her lingering sense of foreboding. Lord Rutherford was a nobleman pursuing some momentary whim, and as long as he provided her with a pound a week and her board, she really did not care too much what that whim might be. Her recent brush with starvation had worked a powerful effect on the ordering of her priorities. It was necessary to eat in order to live, and it was necessary to be alive in order to be virtuous. Her philosophy of life thus satisfactorily settled, she turned to the parcels with renewed enthusiasm.

It was so long since she had worn anything new

that her fingers shook with excitement as she pulled at the knots of string. The first package revealed two sets of sturdy cotton underwear, and a flannel nightgown. A small box contained a pair of brown walking-boots. A larger box held a brown velveteen bonnet, two pairs of woollen stockings and a pair of knitted gloves. A comb and a toothbrush were wrapped up separately in brown paper.

Deborah dressed herself in one set of white underwear, tying a petticoat round her waist with sigh of satisfaction. It felt so solid, so eminently respectable. Surely, if she worked hard . . . if Lord Rutherford was pleased with her . . . he would find her a permanent position with one of his friends. The prospect of permanent employment was so enticing that she had to shut her mind to the possibility. She had learned the danger of allowing herself to dream.

She tied the garters on her stockings and secured the final button on her shift, then turned excitedly to the biggest parcel of all. She quickly unwrapped the two dresses Mrs Bowler had bought for her. One was of grey-brown serge and the other of dark brown brushed wool. The housekeeper, Deborah decided wryly, evidently liked brown.

She quickly dismissed a faint quiver of disappointment. She selected the grey-brown serge as more suitable for travelling, and put on first the bodice, then the matching skirt. Both garments were cut without any particular sense of style and both were far too big for her, but she shivered with happiness as the soft folds of the skirt fell in place over her petticoat. The quality of the cloth was good, and she knew she would be able to alter the dress so that it fit her well. As for style, she had no desire whatsoever to be fashionable. She combed her hair, plaiting it tightly and pinning it in a severe bun at the nape of her neck. She twirled around the tiny room, listening to the gentle swish of her skirt as the fabric twirled with her. She wished very much for a mirror—she would have loved to view her splendid new image. I probably look just like a real housekeeper, she thought.

She joined the servants for lunch, and sat at a table laden with more food than she had seen in a month. She helped herself generously to beef stew and dumplings, followed by rice pudding with hot jam, which she had to eat slowly. Her stomach had shrunk to such an extent that it could no longer accommodate a meal of normal size.

Afterwards, she offered her services to Mrs Bowler, but the housekeeper looked horrified at the thought of unqualified help wandering round her kitchen. 'The boot-boy has taken a carpet-bag to your room, miss. You should pack your spare belongings and then wait there for Lord Rutherford's summons. There is no extra help needed in *my* kitchen.'

Back in her room, Deborah carefully placed the neat packages inside the shabby case, relishing the fact that there was barely room to fit everything in. As she worked, she tunelessly hummed the Jewel Song from Gounod's *Faust*, a new opera which her mother had loved. The more she thought about it, the more fortunate she considered herself to be. She could hardly believe the twists of fate that had

brought her in one day from near starvation to a
point where she required a carpet-bag to contain all
her new and valuable possessions. She was in the
act of buckling on its strap when the kitchen-maid
arrived at her door.

''Is lordship is waiting to leave, miss. He says to
'urry, or you'll miss the train.'

Deborah picked up her bag. It felt wonderfully
heavy, a comforting sign of her affluence. 'I'm
ready,' she said.

Lord Rutherford was already inside his brougham
when Deborah arrived at the front of the house. A
groom immediately took her bag, and helped her
into the carriage. 'We'll put this in the hackney with
his lordship's luggage, miss. You won't want it at
your feet.'

'I suppose not,' she said. She watched a trifle
anxiously as he closed the carriage door and walked
away with her bag. It did, after all, contain the sum
total of her worldly belongings. The coachman set
off at a brisk pace and the footman was lost to view.
Deborah forced all thoughts of the carpet-bag out
of her mind, and looked covertly at her new employer. He was staring out of the carriage window
and, for all his face expressed to the contrary, he
might have been unaware of her presence on the
seat beside him. He had certainly not looked at her
long enough to see her splendid new clothes.
Deborah was aware of a faint stirring of irritation.
She had so hoped he would be impressed by her air
of restrained dowdiness. Surely he ought to be
pleased that she now looked just like any other

housekeeper? She decided to ignore the rule which said that servants could not speak until addressed by their employers.

'Thank you for my new clothes, my lord. It was good of you and your housekeeper to purchase them for me so swiftly.'

His gaze flickered over her for a fraction of a second, then returned to stare out of the window. 'It was a necessary task, as you yourself pointed out this morning.'

The silence returned, and this time it was so absolute that Deborah had no courage to break it. She gave a tiny sigh, not quite sure what was bothering her, then turned and stared out of her window at the busy London scene. It was raining, and people scurried about their business under a protective shield of umbrellas. Carriages were veiled in a misty haze of rain, and the privet hedges seemed momentarily to gleam with the fresh green of springtime instead of the dull grey of October. Deborah smiled faintly. How easy it was to find London attractive when one viewed it from the comfort of a weather-proof carriage!

The Cheltenham train left London from Paddington station, and Deborah realised suddenly that they were driving down the street which contained Mrs Pritchard's boarding-house. She watched intently for the approach of the familiar iron gate, and felt sure she could see a twitch of the stiff lace curtains as the smart brougham rattled past. She almost laughed aloud with the sheer pleasure of being alive and well fed.

She thought for a moment about her despair of

the previous night and was filled with a rush of gratitude towards Lord Rutherford. However forbidding he might seem on the surface, his true character must be generous or he would not have helped her. She turned away from the carriage window to look at him, and was surprised to find him staring at her. For some reason, a faint blush coloured her cheeks, but she nevertheless flashed him dazzling smile of thanks. There was a moment of inexplicable tension in the carriage, then his lips tightened and he looked quickly away.

She dropped her gaze to her lap, folding her hands neatly and rubbing her thumbs over the pleasant roughness of her new woollen gloves. She wished she could find some way to put her gratitude into words, she wished she could share her joy at escaping from Mrs Pritchard's clutches, but she doubted if he would understand her feelings. It was unlikely that so great a nobleman would ever have known a moment of true worry in his life. The carriage came to a swaying halt and the door was pulled open. Deborah saw that they had been driven right on to the departure platform, a privilege accorded only to noblemen and railway company directors.

Several uniformed railway officials bowed as Lord Rutherford emerged from the carriage and exchanged greetings with the station-master. Deborah followed her employer out of the brougham, then hesitated on the platform. Was she supposed to travel with him, or in another compartment of the train?

'Get in,' he said. 'You are holding everything up. The train was only waiting for our arrival in order to depart.'

She hadn't known Lord Rutherford was even watching her, let alone that he was aware of her momentary hesitation. It was disconcerting to think that he was as conscious of her movements as she was of his. She had never experienced this peculiar awareness of another human being before, and couldn't understand what caused it. He gave a small exclamation of impatience and leaned out of the carriage. 'Do hurry up,' he said.

She gathered her skirts tightly around her knees and climbed up the high steps. There was an immediate blast on the guard's whistle and the train jerked into motion, rolling out under the soaring arches of the station.

The dreary outskirts of London had been left behind before Lord Rutherford spoke again. 'Have you travelled by train before?' he asked.

'Yes, my lord. Both here and in Europe.'

'You have travelled on the Continent? With your mother?'

'Yes, my lord. I spent much of my childhood in Italy.'

He asked no further questions. 'The train journey will last for about three and a half hours,' he said. He took a volume from the pocket of his travelling cape and opened it in the middle, frowning slightly as he began to read. The book, Deborah saw, was a copy of Plato's *Dialogues*. His concentration on the philosopher's great thoughts appeared to be absolute, so she wondered why, after half an hour of total silence, he still hadn't remembered to turn the page.

The rain had stopped by the time they arrived in Cheltenham, but it was almost dusk and the October air was chilly. Deborah was glad to wait in the station-master's warm sitting-room while a carriage was summoned to drive them from Cheltenham to the village of Upper Hinsdale.

'We shall be at the cottage in less than an hour,' Lord Rutherford said as soon as they were settled in the hired carriage. 'I regret that there was no time to send a message to notify the staff of our arrival.'

'This carriage is perfectly comfortable,' Deborah said. She leaned forward to look out of the window. 'I have never visited Wiltshire or Gloucestershire. It's very pretty, isn't it? Some of the hills and the copses of small trees look more like a landscaped garden than a natural part of the countryside.'

'The soil in this region is very fertile and it has been cultivated since the Romans first conquered Britain. In truth, you will see very little of nature's unaided work in this part of the country.'

'The people born here are more fortunate than those born in the north. I was noticing during the train journey how rich the farmland looked and how prosperous the villagers appeared. The men were bundled up in warm clothes, and all the children wore shoes. Even the dogs looked well fed!'

'England is the most prosperous country in the world,' he replied, and she could not interpret the curious inflection of his voice. 'Our farms grow more food per acre than any other country in the world, and our factories produce more than the whole of Europe. Why shouldn't the dogs be fat and the children warmly clothed?'

'Why not indeed?' she said bitterly, remembering all too clearly Cousin George's cloth mills and the painfully thin, shoeless children who had worked the looms, their ragged clothes permanently wet with steam. 'But you must forgive my astonishment. I am only a woman and therefore incapable of understanding why national prosperity so often seems to require that children should go hungry.'

She felt his immediate spark of interest and she thought he was going to question her further, probing the unspoken anger of her response, but in the end he said nothing. He leaned back in his seat and closed his eyes. When he looked at her again, his expression was so tightly shuttered that no trace of interest or emotion was discernible. Nothing more was said until the carriage rumbled through the cobbled streets of a small village, and then he spoke without even turning to glance out of the window.

'Hinsdale Cottage is on the crest of the next rise,' he said. 'We shall be there in five minutes.'

Deborah saw that his hands tightened round the knob of his cane, although his voice sounded entirely devoid of feeling. A few months ago, she would have heard only the flatness of his voice and never noticed the betraying tension of his hands. Two months of living on the edge of starvation had sharpened her perceptions. She wondered why a visit to one of his country houses should cause Lord Rutherford to pretend a calm he did not feel, but excitement at their imminent arrival pushed the thought to the back of her mind. She peered intently out of the carriage window. She could see little through the darkness save the shadow of a large building and the glow of two or three faint lights.

'It is very imposing for a cottage,' she said as they passed through the arched entrance to a long driveway.

'It is more a manor house than a cottage. It was rebuilt at the end of the seventeenth century when Charles II returned some land to the Hinsdale family as a reward for their loyalty during the war with Oliver Cromwell. For some reason, the original name of the property has never been changed.'

'Has the cottage always been in your family's possession?' Deborah asked. 'Are the Hinsdales a branch of the Rutherford family?'

'No,' he said. 'My father purchased the property in 1848, three years before he died.' After a pause he added, 'He . . . my father . . . lived here during the final two years of his life. It is a very . . . secluded . . . property.'

The carriage drew to a halt. Lord Rutherford climbed out without waiting for the coachman to open the door, then turned to help Deborah to descend. He stared into the distance as she placed her gloved hand on his arm and stepped down. They moved quickly away from each other as soon as she had both feet on the cobblestones.

While Lord Rutherford paid the coachman, she looked round the unlit courtyard and was struck by the many signs of neglect. Weeds grew between cracks in the paving, and the cobblestones were mossy. Even in the darkness she could see that the hedges surrounding the courtyard were wildly overgrown and liberally interspersed with brambles. Although there were lights in the house, and the iron wheels of the coach had made a great deal of noise crossing the courtyard, there was still no sign of a servant hurrying to unbar the front door.

The coachman was sent to knock on the weather-stained oak door. Lord Rutherford's gaze never left the man, but he extended his arm in Deborah's direction. 'These slippery cobblestones are hazardous, Miss Phipps. Perhaps you would care for some assistance?'

'Oh, no, thank you, my lord,' she said hurriedly. For some reason, she was loath to come into physical contact with her employer. She smiled brightly, although he still didn't seem to be looking at her. 'I can do very well by myself, thank you.' She had not taken more than a couple of steps before she was forced to clutch his sleeve in order to avoid falling. He waited without speaking while she regained her footing, and then silently tucked her hand under his arm. Deborah found that her legs were shaking, a condition she ascribed to her stumble, since she could think of no other explanation for this uncharacteristic display of feminine weakness.

The coachman's pounding on the knocker achieved success just as they arrived at the entrance to the cottage. An old man, dressed more like a groom than a butler, opened the door to reveal a dimly-lit hallway. Two elderly women hovered nervously in the background.

' 'Tis 'is lordship!' one of the women gasped. ' 'Tis 'im!'

The male servant tried unsuccessfully to unroll his shirt-sleeves and button his jerkin both at the same time. 'Would you care to step inside, my lord? I'm right sorry. We wasn't expecting you . . . We hadn't a message . . '

'There was no time to send one,' Lord Rutherford said. He dismissed the coachman with an instruction concerning the luggage, then walked into the oak-panelled hallway of the cottage. Deborah slowly followed him.

Her first impression was one of awe. The hallway was beautifully proportioned and exquisitely panelled. A massive stairway curved graciously to one side, its banisters carved in a delicate design of twining roses. Her second impression was one of shocked disbelief at the total neglect everywhere in evidence. The panelling was cracked and dull from lack of polish. As they walked further into the hallway, dirt and dry leaves crunched underfoot. The manservant conducted them to a formal drawing-room, its furniture wrapped in dust-sheets, but when he lit the wall lamps, Deborah saw that a magnificent crystal chandelier hung unprotected from the centre of the painted ceiling, its lustres greasy with stale candle-wax.

Lord Rutherford stripped off his gloves, not bothering to look round the room. 'How are you, Jenkins?'

'Well, I'm well, my lord. But we wasn't expecting

your lordship. Nobody sent us word from London.'

'No, as I mentioned, we did not have time to notify you of our impending arrival. I'm glad that you are well. I trust your son is enjoying his work in Bristol?'

'Yes, he is that, my lord. It's a real pleasure to have a book-keeper in the family. His mother would be proud. Er . . . Is your lordship planning to stay for long? And the young lady . . . ?'

'I'm not sure as yet. We shall need a fire in here, Jenkins. And in our bedrooms, too, I've no doubt.'

'Yes, m'lord.'

'Perhaps you would send the housekeeper to escort Miss Phipps to the Rose Room? And we shall require dinner as soon as cook can prepare something. Do you think she could manage to serve us within the hour?'

'Yes, my lord, I dare say. Of course we wasn't expecting your lordship. We never had a message . . .' His voice tailed into unhappy silence.

'I believe that Miss Phipps and I have both grasped the unfortunate fact that our arrival is unexpected, Jenkins, but I am not requesting a banquet. Merely a light meal and two or three fires. I shall also require some hot water in my room as soon as you can attend to it.'

'Yes, my lord.'

Lord Rutherford turned to leave. He had not once looked in Deborah's direction since entering the house. 'Oh, do not forget the housekeeper will be needed to escort Miss Phipps.'

One of the elderly female servants stepped out of

the shadows in the hallway where she had been hovering. 'I be here already, your lordship.'

Deborah thought that the coldness of Lord Rutherford's eyes warmed for a second or two. 'Hello, Mrs Potter, I did not see you there. How are you keeping? It looks to me as if you are doing better than ever.'

'I'm not so bad, my lord.' Mrs Potter tried to bob into a curtsy as she spoke. The generous flow of her curves made the exercise difficult and her double chin wobbled as she smiled. 'It's good to have you here, my lord. It's been too long since you paid us a visit. Not since your poor father died, and that's nigh on thirteen years . . .'

The warmth instantly vanished from Lord Rutherford's eyes. 'Yes,' he said. He strode quickly from the room, pausing only when he reached the staircase. 'Miss Phipps is no doubt tired after her journey. I know you will do your best to make her comfortable.' He went swiftly upstairs, and disappeared into the gloomy reaches of the upper hall.

After a moment of uneasy silence, the housekeeper conducted Deborah to an imposing bedroom on the first floor. The walls were covered in faded pink silk, and the velvet bed-hangings were of the same colour. The furniture here was also swathed in dust-sheets, but the housekeeper pulled the protective coverings from a comfortable chair and indicated that Deborah should sit down.

'This is the Rose Room, miss. Some water will be sent up for you.'

'I can easily come down and fetch it myself,'

Deborah said. 'I know that our unexpected arrival must make things difficult for you.'

'Better you stay up here, miss. Jenkins will be going crazy in the kitchen. We're not used to making meals for visitors. We weren't expecting the young master at all.'

Deborah could see that her own unexplained presence was of no significance at all in comparison to the arrival of Lord Rutherford. She had wondered if the servants here would treat her with scorn or suspicion, but such worries had clearly been a waste of time. She smiled at the houskeeper, trying to offer reassurance. All the staff seemed so flustered that she felt obliged to put them at their ease, almost as if she were their mistress rather than a junior servant.

'I shall rest here quite comfortably until the water arrives. Take your time, Mrs Potter.'

The housekeeper made another tottering attempt at a curtsy and then departed, leaving Deborah free to examine the faded grandeur of her bedroom. With some trepidation, she turned back the covers of the bed. Clouds of dust blew up, thick enough to be visible even by candlelight, but she was relieved to note that no horrid scurryings accompanied her action. Apparently there had been no food left in the room to attract mice or rats.

She had not quite finished removing dust-covers when a tall, powerfully built manservant arrived carrying a jug of hot water. A towel and a set of bed-linen were tossed over his shoulder. A quick search of the room failed to unearth a washbasin,

and the hapless servant had forgotten the soap, but
Deborah managed to reassure him that she would
wash directly from the jug. Since the water was so
hot, she would make do without soap. He sighed
with unfeigned relief and she began to wonder why,
in a household where she had already seen four
servants, the simplest housekeeping chores seemed
to present such problems.

She made up the bed with the clean sheets, which
were yellowed along the folds but thankfully not at
all damp. She then removed her clothes and shook
the travel dust from them, and washed as well as
she could. When she had dressed, she thought an
hour had probably gone by, so she walked downstairs to the drawing-room.

Lord Rutherford was already in the room, standing in front of the empty fireplace. The covers had
been removed from two chairs, and a small boulle
table pulled close to the non-existent fire. A half-
full decanter and one glass reposed on a tarnished
silver tray on top of the table. As she entered the
drawing-room, Lord Rutherford lifted the glass to
her in a mocking salute.

'How do you like the Rose Room, Miss Phipps?
An elegant boudoir, is it not?'

'It is a trifle dusty, my lord, but I imagine it could
be made into an attractive bedroom.'

'A suitable setting for your beauty, perhaps?'
Lord Rutherford took another generous swallow
from his glass, and Deborah felt a moment of fear.
Was this, perhaps, the hidden truth about her
employer? That he was a drunkard who needed to
hide himself from his friends?

'I am not drunk,' he said, proving once again his uncanny ability to read her thoughts. 'You would do well to remember that it is you, Miss Phipps, who have yet to show that you can remain sober. I, unfortunately, have a very hard head and cannot retreat from my problems into the pleasures of a drink-sodden dream.'

'I did not accuse you of drunkenness, my lord.'

'But it was in your eyes, Miss Phipps. Did your opera-singer mother never tell you that you have speaking eyes?'

Jenkins arrived in the doorway, saving her from the embarrassment of finding a suitable reply. 'Dinner is served, my lord, but the dining-room chimney was smoking and we had to put out the fire.'

'It doesn't matter. I had not expected to find comfort in this house.'

The dining-room was on the same massive scale as the rest of the house, and the table could easily have seated thirty people. The dust-sheets had been rolled back from only one end of it and had been replaced by a small cloth that was not large enough to conceal several inches of unpolished wood. Lord Rutherford seated himself in the carved oaken chair at the head of the table. He paid no attention to the lack of polish or the wisps of wood-smoke still circling the room.

'Do you wish me to eat with you?' Deborah enquired softly. 'I had expected to eat in the kitchen. I am a servant, after all.'

'You will eat with me,' he said curtly. 'You may serve, Jenkins.'

The butler, for such Deborah had now decided he must be, went to the doorway and summoned assistance. The housekeeper carried in two bowls of soup and handed them to the butler. 'Mutton broth,' she said in a penetrating whisper.

The absurdity of the whole situation suddenly struck Deborah with full force and she had to take a large gulp of water in order to control her giggles. Mrs Bowler would have apoplexy if any of these servants had ever worked in her kitchen. The butler placed the soup in front of her as soon as she put down her glass.

The thin grey liquid looked excessively unappealing, but at least steam still rose from it, indicating that it would provide some warmth to counteract the icy chill of the unheated room. With only a momentary hesitation, Deborah picked up her soup-spoon.

She had taken no more than three small mouthfuls when she became aware that Lord Rutherford was observing her every movement with the most intense concentration. All through their journey from London he had studiously avoided so much as a glance in her direction. Now he allowed his own food to grow cold while he watched her. What on earth, Deborah thought, could be so fascinating about watching somebody consume watery mutton soup? She put down her spoon, and touched her mouth lightly with her napkin. 'You do not find the broth to your liking, my lord?' she enquired innocently.

'I am not particularly hungry,' he said.

His curtness for some reason provoked her. She

laughed the silvery little laugh which had always made Cousin George's elderly friends pat her hand with avuncular affection. 'I am blessed with the most fortunate of constitutions,' she said. 'Travel, whether by train or coach, rarely seems to affect my appetite.' She smiled at him again and returned to her soup, managing to finish almost all of it despite his unwinking stare. Jenkins ordered the removal of their soup-plates, and Lord Rutherford seemed temporarily to lose interest in Deborah. He requested a glass of burgundy, but when the butler would have poured some wine into Deborah's glass, he was told firmly that Miss Phipps did not drink any alcoholic beverages.

The broth was eventually replaced by a platter of unidentifiable cold meat and two dishes of reheated vegetables. One vegetable was green (possibly cabbage?) and the other was orange (carrots? swedes?). When the butler held out the serving-platters, Deborah prudently helped herself with extreme caution.

The caution proved to be entirely justified. The food was inedible. Deborah quickly abandoned the effort to swallow gristly meat and wooden vegetables, reflecting as she did so that only two days ago she would have been grateful to eat what she now rejected. The thought was a sobering one, and she scarcely registered that once again Lord Rutherford was observing her most minute actions.

After the disaster of the second course, Jenkins's manner was even more uncertain when he carried in the dessert. 'There was no time to prepare anything fancy,' he said. 'There is cheese, my lord, and apples from the orchard if Miss Phipps would care for something sweet.'

'An apple is just what I should like,' Deborah said, feeling sorry for Jenkins, who was not, after all, responsible for the cook's shortcomings. The butler smiled at her gratefully as he brought the dish of fruit to her. 'The apples has been lovely this year, miss. That red one will be as sweet as you could wish for.'

'Thank you.' Deborah took the apple and waited for Lord Rutherford to help himself to a small portion of cheese. She peeled and ate the apple, refusing to pay any attention to Lord Rutherford's glowering presence at the head of the table.

'Do you wish for coffee in the drawing-room, miss?' Jenkins asked when she had finished eating.

She was not given the chance to reply. 'Miss Phipps is tired and wishes to go to her room. Please ask Mrs Potter to escort her.'

Deborah, reminding herself that Lord Rutherford was paying her one pound a week to tolerate his moods, simply smiled at Jenkins and waited for him to pull out her chair. 'There is no need to disturb Mrs Potter,' she said. 'I know how busy she must be with our unexpected arrival. Goodnight, my lord. And thank you, Jenkins, for helping me to select such a delicious apple.'

'It was a pleasure, miss. We'll try to do better with the meals tomorrow, miss.'

Lord Rutherford stood up, pushing aside his chair with a distinct clatter. 'I will take brandy in the drawing-room now, Jenkins.' He strode out of the room and Deborah quietly followed. The butler stopped her at the foot of the stairs.

'Goodnight, miss,' he said. 'His lordship's bark is worse than his bite, miss. It always has been, ever since he was a lad. A fine man, his lordship, a very fine man.'

'I'm sure he is,' Deborah said, and wished that she were absolutely certain she was speaking the truth.

CHAPTER
FIVE

DESPITE JENKINS'S promises, breakfast next morning was not much better than the previous night's dinner, and the dining-room looked more neglected than ever in the bright morning sun.

Lord Rutherford glowered silently throughout the meal, but Deborah refused to share in his gloom. She had slept deeply, untroubled by the dust and faded grandeur of her bedroom, and had woken full of renewed energy and goodwill. After two days of adequate food, she was disposed to be charitable towards all mankind, even Lord Rutherford who, no doubt, had excellent reasons for his seemingly inexplicable behaviour.

Deborah's cheerfulness survived unscathed while she ate two undercooked eggs and a slice of withered ham. As she buttered her second slice of burned toast, however, she began to wonder why Lord Rutherford insisted that she must sit at his table, since he did nothing but glare at her. She decided that she would not be intimidated by his deepening frown. For the second time since her arrival at Hinsdale Cottage, she reminded herself that he was paying a pound a week for the privilege of scowling at her (not to mention a five-pound bonus at the end of her stay). Keeping the thought of such largesse in mind, she didn't find it at all difficult to return each of his scowls with a friendly smile.

As soon as she had swallowed her last mouthful of toast, Lord Rutherford stood up. 'Have you finally finished eating, Miss Phipps?'

'Yes, thank you, my lord.'

'I have business to transact which will take me away from the estate for the rest of the day. I will bid you good morning.'

'But, my lord, you have given me no instructions concerning my work! What would you like me to do while you are gone?'

He scarcely paused in his march to the front door. 'Whatever you please,' he said. 'It is of no consequence to me.'

Deborah resisted an impulse to pull a most un-ladylike face at his retreating back. If Lord Rutherford wanted to waste his money employing her to do nothing he was perfectly entitled to do so, but she did wish he had appointed her to some quite normal position such as housekeeper or upstairs maid. How could she earn her keep if she was given no duties?

When Lord Rutherford had left, she decided to explore the extensive grounds and went up to her room to fetch her old cloak before walking out into the October sunshine. It felt wonderful to breathe the clear air of the countryside after so many weeks in London. She wandered round the gardens, which once had obviously been well laid out and lovingly tended, although now they were as neglected as the house.

Lord Rutherford seemed to hate the cottage, and the ageing servants had gradually allowed everything to slide into a state of disrepair. But if he disliked the property that much, why didn't he sell it?

She came to a high wall of mellowed yellow brick and trailed her hand along the rough surface, feeling the warmth of the autumn sun soaking into the brick. She lifted her face up to the sky, revelling for a moment in the touch of the sun on her skin and hair. A wicket-gate gave her access to the remains of a flourishing herb-garden, but only a few straggly shoots of parsley and some overgrown clumps of mint remained.

She picked a shoot of mint and sniffed at its fragrant leaves as she walked back to the house. She entered through a side door which led straight into the servants' quarters. In this part of the house, everything was in a reasonable state of repair. The floors were scrubbed and the sun shone through clean windows. The still-room and the laundry appeared well organised and the pantry was adequately stocked with essential supplies. She was on the point of returning to her bedroom when she heard a low murmur of voices coming from the kitchen and, on an impulse, she opened the door and went in.

The housekeeper was peeling turnips at a large wooden table, and the butler, up to his elbows in soapy water, was scrubbing pots. There were no other servants in the room. The cheerful buzz of their conversation halted abruptly as Deborah entered the kitchen, and she spoke quickly to cover the embarrassing silence. 'I have come to see if there is some way I can help,' she said. 'I know how difficult it must be for you to have Lord Rutherford arrive unexpectedly after such a long absence.'

'Thirteen years come Michaelmas,' Jenkins said. 'That's when his father died. The master hasn't been here since then.'

'That is certainly a long time. I wonder why it has been so long?'

'I couldn't say, miss, I'm sure. Was there something special you wished for, miss?'

'No, no,' she said hurriedly, sensing Jenkins's resistance to any questions about his master. 'But where are the other servants? Lord Rutherford said there were five or six people employed here, not counting the stable lads and the gardeners.'

'We're only four servants now,' the housekeeper replied. 'And no lads in the stables, either. There's just Martha and Will apart from us two. Martha's cleaning up the dining-room and Will is out seeing to the horses. You'll meet him later, I dare say. And you know Jenkins and me, miss. Jenkins is the butler and I'm the cook, more or less.'

'But, last night, Lord Rutherford said you were the housekeeper,' Deborah exclaimed.

'I'm cook and housekeeper, too,' Mrs Potter said. 'But I wasn't trained for either job, that's the problem. I was midwife to her ladyship at the start, and then I had to come and look after his lordship, the old lord . . .'

Jenkins interrupted. 'The cook died, miss. That

was five years ago, and there weren't no cause to replace her, seeing as how neither his lordship nor his mother ever came to stay here.'

Deborah wondered if she imagined the brief flash of warning that he directed at Mrs Potter. For whatever reason, the housekeeper's moment of loquacity was over. She returned to her silent peeling of turnips, and Deborah, contemplating several more weeks of Mrs Potter's cooking, decided that the moment had come to take action. 'You have all done a wonderful job of keeping everything running smoothly,' she said. 'But it seems to me there are a lot of things we must do if Hinsdale Cottage is to be made comfortable for your master. First of all, we must see about getting you some extra help in the kitchen. Lord Rutherford, I'm sure, has no idea how hard you are all having to work.'

'I don't know, miss,' Jenkins said. 'His lordship didn't authorise . . .'

'Lord Rutherford told me that I might do whatever I pleased.' Deborah hoped she sounded more sure of herself than she felt. 'And I am sure he would be very worried if he knew how overworked you all are.'

'I suppose Will could ride into the village when he's finished with the horses,' said the butler. 'He could find a couple of sturdy girls from a respectable family. The extra help would make a big difference, miss. We're none of us getting any younger, and that's a fact.'

'I am sure Lord Rutherford will be delighted to have the household organised so quickly,' Deborah said. She saw that this remark was a clincher as far as the butler was concerned, and concealed a sigh of relief under a friendly smile. She had dealt with enough elderly servants in Cousin George's house to know that decisiveness was essential if anything was ever to change.

'How soon would you like to have your luncheon, miss?' Mrs Potter asked.

'I will just have some fruit,' she said. 'I can eat it here, if I am not too much in your way. And this afternoon, while Will is riding into the village, perhaps Martha could help me to arrange my bedroom? In that way, Mrs Potter, you and Jenkins will have all afternoon free to prepare Lord Rutherford's dinner.'

'Yes, miss. We'll see about it right away.'

Deborah and Martha started on the mammoth task of cleaning her bedroom immediately after lunch. They worked furiously through the early hours of the afternoon, dusting and washing and polishing until the furniture gleamed and the whole room smelled sweetly of lavender and beeswax. In the late afternoon, Will, who had returned from the village with two additional serving-maids, carried up three steaming copper cans of hot water and Deborah was able both to have a bath and to wash her hair. Two baths in two days, she thought, with a silent laugh that hovered somewhere between wryness and happiness. I shall have to be careful not to become accustomed to such luxuries!

After her bath, she changed into the second of her new dresses, of dark brown wool and, although she knew it could never be termed a glamorous ensemble, she was well pleased with the overall effect. The severe style made her look dignified, she decided, and older than her nineteen years.

Her hair was much less satisfactory than her new dress. The thick newly-washed curls rioted over her shoulders in a hopeless profusion of shining chestnut. After struggling for more than twenty minutes, Deborah gave up the hopeless attempt to produce a tight braid and coiled the unruly mass into a loose knot at the nape of her neck. There was nothing to be done about the tiny curls left framing her face except to tuck them behind her ears and hope that his lordship wouldn't notice. They definitely spoiled her image as a cool, mature female eminently suited to superior domestic service.

Just as she was preparing to leave her bedroom, she heard Lord Rutherford's firm tread taking the stairs two at a time, and then moving quickly along the corridor to his bedroom. She couldn't account for the little burst of pleasure that quickened her pulses. She waited until she heard his door close, then ran quickly down the stairs into the garden, searching through the overgrown flowerbeds until she found some purple daisies and late-blooming marigolds. Returning to the house, she arranged the flowers in a silver bowl, then carefully set the arrangement in the middle of the dining-table, where they made the perfect finishing touch.

She could see that Jenkins and Martha had worked hard. The polished mahogany of the table now groaned under enough porcelain, silver and crystal to please the most demanding mistress. The

chimney was no longer smoking and the fire suf-
fused the room with a soothing yellow glow, en-
hancing the deep orange of the marigolds and the
rich purple of the daisies. She gave a tiny sigh of
contentment, then looked up, startled, when she
heard a faint rustle of movement in the doorway.
Lord Rutherford stood there, resplendent in formal evening clothes. It was a moment before she
could recover her breath.

'G-good evening,' she said, wondering why her
voice sounded so strange to her own ears. 'I hope
you had a successful day?'

'Thank you, yes.'

'I . . . I was checking to see that the table was in
order. Jenkins and Mrs Potter have done an excellent job, haven't they?'

'Excellent,' he said. She supposed he must have
looked at the table, although in the dim light she
could have sworn his eyes never left her face. 'If
you will excuse me, I shall tell Jenkins we are ready
to eat. There is a bell near the fireplace, but I doubt
very much if it's working.'

At first she thought that dinner was to be a repeat
of the other gloomy meals they had shared. The
food was not well prepared, and Lord Rutherford
responded to Deborah's efforts at conversation
with little more than curt monosyllables. She was
on the point of giving up her attempts to keep the
conversation going when, in answer to a casual
question about employment in the village, he suddenly began to speak of his day's activities.

'I have been on a tour of some factories,' he said.
'Many of the villagers work in the local woollen

mills. Hinsdale has been a sheep-farming region for centuries, and there has always been a certain amount of woollen cloth produced here. In my grandfather's day, I believe there were many skilled handloom weavers earning a good living from the cloth they wove in their own cottages. Of course, small factories took over from the handloom weaves more than a generation ago.' He broke off. 'I beg your pardon,' he said. 'I must be boring you. I am sure you are not interested in the development of the Cotswold woollen industry. It is not a subject likely to entertain the feminine mind.'

'On the contrary, my lord,' she replied calmly. 'I have some familiarity with the cotton-manufacturing industry in the north, and I am deeply interested in what you have to say.'

'Oh, of course. You mentioned that you had lived in the north. Did you work in a cotton mill?'

'Not . . . not exactly. I simply visited one or two. But please tell me more about your tour, my lord.'

He looked at her closely for several tense seconds then, with a brief gesture, he indicated that the butler should refill his wineglass. 'My first impression was that the conditions in the mills were not too bad," he said. 'I thought the weavers looked tired, particularly the young girls, but the owners seemed decent men and the buildings had been constructed with some thought for the health and safety of the workers. The lighting was adequate and there was decent ventilation. But I soon discovered that the accident rate is appallingly

high, and when I persuaded the owners to talk
more freely, I found out that the competition in
woollen cloth manufacture is so fierce that they
cannot hope to make a profit unless their looms are
working twelve hours a day, six days a week. Most
of the women and even some of the children spend
seventy-two hours a week at their jobs. By Saturday night, the younger children are frequently too
tired to jump out of the path of moving machin-
ery—hence the high rate of accidents.'

The pictures conjured up by his words were
disturbingly vivid, and Deborah couldn't repress a
shudder. She had seen too many limbs mangled by
the downthrust of Cousin George's giant looms. 'It
is terrible when young children must work to the
point of exhaustion,' she said. 'I have heard so
often that there is nothing to be done about it. Do
you think that is true?'

'Of course it is not,' he said. 'There is always
some solution to problems if only we are prepared
to look hard enough. For the past few weeks I have
been working on the draft of a new Bill to come
before Parliament. The Bill seeks to extend the
provisions of the Factory Acts to cover the small
factories which at present are outside the scope of
the law, such as all the little mills I visited today
and many others like them. It would, in effect,
guarantee a sixty-hour week and ensure that
honest factory-owners are not forced to exploit
their workers.'

'I understand,' Deborah said thoughtfully. 'If the
law limits the number of hours that people may
work, then owners cannot reduce their costs by

making weavers work fourteen hours a day for no extra pay. The honest owners, who wish to pay a fair wage, are thus protected from their more cut-throat competitors. When I lived in the north, I realised that if one cruel employer kept his prices low by exploiting his workers, the honest owner was forced to do the same or find himself priced out of his market.'

Lord Rutherford appeared startled. 'You have summed up the situation with admirable clarity, Miss Phipps. If only my colleagues in the House of Lords could find it equally easy to understand my arguments on this subject! I have moments when I wonder if some of my noble colleagues understand *any* subject which is more complex than the breeding schedule of their horses.'

Deborah tried not to blush. Breeding was a subject she had never heard mentioned before, even in relation to horses. 'I hope your Bill will include provisions for more inspectors,' she said. 'It is all very well saying that women and children may work only ten and a half hours a day, and no more than sixty hours in one week. But if there are no inspectors to see that the law is carried out, then it is not worth the paper it is printed on.'

'Indeed, and so I have frequently remarked myself. Inspectors are the key to success in factory legislation.' Lord Rutherford fell abruptly silent. 'When did you become so well conversant with the problems of factory operatives?' he asked. 'You are sure you have never worked in a factory?'

'No, my lord, I have never worked in a factory, but in Yorkshire everybody knows about conditions in the cloth mills. And, of course, I have read newspaper accounts of the debates in Parliament.'

'Of course,' he said sarcastically. 'In *The Times*, no doubt.'

'Yes, my lord, and in the *Manchester Guardian* when I have been able to find a copy.'

She saw the curiosity in his eyes and realised that her remarks had aroused his interest. Until this moment he had no doubt assumed that she was illiterate. He deliberately cut off his questions, however, perhaps because of the servants, and the spark of warmth and liveliness vanished from his expression. He stood up, and she saw that his features were once again arranged into a cool mask of reserve, tinged with a hint of scorn. 'I know you will excuse me, Miss Phipps, even though you have not yet finished your dinner. I have urgent work to complete this evening.'

She smothered an irrational feeling of disappointment. 'Certainly, my lord. But could you please tell me precisely what I am expected to do tomorrow? I hope, my lord, that you have found everything satisfactory so far?'

'Satisfactory?' he repeated with a small, harsh laugh. 'Oh yes, Miss Phipps, everything about you is eminently satisfactory.' He touched his hand to his forehead and for a moment there was a whiteness to the taut, controlled line of his mouth. 'I think we shall discuss your job in the morning,' he said. 'I do not find it a convenient subject to discuss at the moment. Good evening, Miss Phipps.' He walked quickly towards the dining-room door.

'Brandy,' he ordered Jenkins. 'Bring it to my study immediately.'

The sound of his footsteps faded rapidly into the distance, and Deborah was left alone to contemplate a dish of custard that had suddenly lost all its appeal.

By mid-morning the next day, Lord Rutherford had still not put in an appearance. Deborah, on tenterhooks for the interview that would finally outline her duties, filled in her time by taking charge of the kitchen. Mrs Potter showed no signs of offence when Deborah helped her prepare a fricassee of chicken for the evening meal, and Jenkins seemed perfectly happy to accept her advice on how the cleaning of the cottage could best be organised. 'I was never trained to be a butler,' he confided as Deborah set the two village girls to beating the drawing-room carpets. 'I was a groom, you see, until the old lord needed me here. They needed somebody strong.'

Such remarks did nothing to appease Deborah's growing curiosity. She ought to have been satisfied to see Hinsdale Cottage slowly return to warm and glowing life, but she felt strangely restless. At lunch-time, she asked Jenkins point-blank where his master had gone.

'He hasn't gone anywhere,' the butler replied. 'As far as I know, miss, his lordship hasn't left his bedroom. He gave orders last night that he weren't to be disturbed until he rang, miss. And he hasn't rung this morning, so naturally we haven't seen him.'

'But he cannot have meant you to leave him sleeping all afternoon!'

Jenkins's pleasant features assumed the mulish expression that was becoming only too familiar. 'Perhaps his lordship feels tired, miss. I would certainly not wish to awaken him.'

By late afternoon Lord Rutherford had still not come downstairs, and his bell remained obstinately silent. Deborah's original irritation had long since given way to a faint but persistent sensation of uneasiness. Although she had known him for such a short time, she felt that her employer was a man of great physical energy and considerable intellectual power. It did not seem to her at all likely that such a man would retreat to bed for the best part of eighteen hours without so much as a request for a glass of fresh water or a light to read by. Unless, she thought, the servants are trying to conceal the truth from me. She remembered his demand for brandy and wondered if he was, in fact, stretched out in a drunken stupor upon his bed.

As the hour for dinner approached, Deborah overrode the half-hearted objections of the servants and announced that she was going to take hot water and a meal up to his lordship's bedroom. She arranged a plate of chicken fricassee and a baked apple on a silver tray and added a pot of fresh coffee. She herself carried the meal upstairs while Martha trailed reluctantly behind, holding the kettle of boiling water and a small oil-lamp. Deborah tapped lightly on the panels of Lord Rutherford's door and waited in some trepidation for his response.

The chicken began to cool, and still she had received no answer. She tapped again, more firmly than before, and heard a faint command to enter. She pushed open the door and slipped quietly inside.

There was almost no light in the room, and she took the small lamp from Martha. The thick curtains were tightly closed and the fire, presumably lit the night before, was now no more than a heap of grey ash. The air struck increasingly chill as she neared the large bed, which was raised on a dais and draped in faded grey damask. Lord Rutherford lay utterly still, his body a rigid hump outlined against the woollen blankets.

She walked over to the dais and quietly set the tray down on a small bedside table. Her heart raced with the beginnings of real fear. He was so still . . . but surely he had ordered her to come in, even though the command had been spoken softly. 'It is dinner-time, my lord,' she said, keeping her voice low. 'I have brought you something to eat.'

'I did not ask for dinner,' he said harshly. 'Get out.'

Martha needed no further encouragement to flee. She deposited her can of hot water in the hearth with a distinct clatter, and hurried out.

Deborah's instinct was to follow suit, but some impulse made her look more closely at Lord Rutherford's unmoving form. His face, in so far as she could judge in the semi-darkness, was rigid with controlled anguish. His complexion, perhaps because of some trick of the lamplight, appeared grey. There was no mistaking the beads of sweat that stood out upon his forehead.

'You are not well,' she said. 'Please allow me to make you more comfortable.'

'I need nothing,' he said. 'Leave me. At once.'

She got as far as his bedroom door before some inexplicable awareness of his pain halted her departure. She turned in the doorway, holding the lamp high, and saw that he was watching her, his eyes dark with pain. Hesitantly, she returned to his side. He quickly shut his eyes, but not before she had noticed the bleakness hovering in their depths. It was almost as if, in addition to the physical hurt, he suffered some haunting mental agony.

'Let me help you,' she said softly, only partly aware of the ambiguous nature of her words.

He did not open his eyes. 'Perhaps some water,' he said at last. There was a carafe of water on a table close to the bed, reinforcing her impression that his pain must be acute if he could not even reach out to it. She poured the water and held the glass out to him.

'Your drink, my lord,' she murmured. She saw his hands clutch the bedclothes as he levered himself on to one elbow, and his knuckles gleamed white with the effort of concealing his discomfort. He took the glass from her and sipped thirstily at the tepid water.

'Lord Rutherford, this room is very cold,' she said. 'Do I have your permission to relight the fire?'

He spoke through clenched teeth. 'If you wish.'

She managed to smooth the pillows before he collapsed back against them, his hand over his eyes to protect them from the faint light of her lamp. She left his room, moving as quietly as she could, and returned to the kitchen.

'Lord Rutherford is not well,' she said to the servants. 'I believe he has a severe headache.' She saw the covert glances the elderly servants exchanged, and she could have sworn she detected a flash of fear in the old housekeeper's eyes. Jenkins cleared his throat. 'Is . . . er . . . is his lordship resting peaceful, miss?'

She looked at the butler narrowly, trying to understand the tension behind his simple question. 'I would imagine that he is resting most unpeacefully,' she said finally. 'His bedroom is cold and gloomy enough to make even a healthy man feel ill. Perhaps you could relight the fire, Jenkins, but take care not to make any noise. My mother was subject to sick headaches of this sort, and I know that the slightest noise could cause her great pain.'

'Yes, miss.' Jenkins hesitated for a moment. 'I'll take the coals up right away,' he said. 'Is there anything else we could do?'

'You could stop looking so down-hearted,' Deborah said with determined cheerfulness. 'Your master has a severe headache, but he is not at death's door, you know.'

Martha and Mrs Potter both seemed to swallow a gasp. 'No, miss. I'm sure you're right,' the housekeeper said.

The fire was already lit when she returned to

Lord Rutherford's room, carrying a drink of weak tea sweetened with honey. The leaping yellow flames and the steady crackle of the coals did much to dispel the dank cheerfulness of the atmosphere. Jenkins had removed the tray of food, but the kettle of hot water remained and she dipped a small towel into it, wringing it out until it was almost dry. She walked quietly to the bed.

'Your headache will be less painful if I may put this towel on your forehead.'

'I don't have a headache,' he snapped.

She did not argue, but simply leaned forward and gently placed the warmth of the towel against his head, wiping away the cold sweat as she did so. She noticed the faintest softening in the lines of pain around his mouth. 'I have some sweet tea in this cup, my lord. If you would drink it, I think you would find it soothing.'

'Dammit, I'm not an invalid! There is nothing wrong with me and I don't need you to play ministering angel!' He jerked angrily away from her touch, then winced as a spasm of pain belied his words. He sank back against the pillows, tearing the towel from his head.

Deborah simply held out the cup. 'Try it, my lord, please. You will find that it tastes good.'

'Give me the damn stuff!' He sipped reluctantly, but he finished all the tea, and Deborah saw to her relief that a faint tinge of colour began to replace the sickly grey pallor of his cheeks. She placed the lamp on a low table so that it cast its circle of light below the level of his eyes and pulled a small screen in front of the fire to shade the flames from his direct line of vision. When she looked at him again, his hands had relaxed their frantic grip on the white linen sheet, and she saw that he was genuinely asleep. She slipped quietly from the room.

She woke soon after dawn the next morning, and crept softly into Lord Rutherford's bedroom. His eyes were closed, but she could tell from the absolute rigidity of his body that he was not sleeping and that he was still in great pain. She started to leave the room, planning to prepare a fresh drink, when he spoke to her, his voice hoarse and faintly pleading.

'Miss Phipps—don't go.'

She had the extraordinary sensation that her heart stopped beating for a moment before it resumed its regular rhythm. She walked slowly back to his bedside, her hands clasped tightly in front of her. 'I shall return as soon as I have made you something to drink,' she said. 'And if Jenkins is up, I will ask him to tend to your fire. Would you like me to open the curtains since you are now awake? I'll draw them back as quietly as I can.'

He did not look at her. 'The light is . . . painful . . .' he admitted.

'Then I will open the curtains only a mere crack, so that there will be just enough light to prevent me banging into the furniture.'

He didn't reply, but she thought that the rigidity of his body relaxed a fraction. This time, he made no protest when she left the room.

The servants were all huddled round the table when she arrived in the kitchen, but the urgent mutter of their voices stopped the moment she walked through the door.

'Good morning,' she said, as four flustered faces stared up at her. 'You are all up bright and early today.'

'Yes, miss. Is there anything we can do for 'is lordship?' Jenkins asked.

Deborah smiled. 'Somebody could build up his fire,' she said. 'I have come to make him some more tea. He is still in considerable pain, however, and I think we should send for the doctor.'

There was another tiny, unnatural silence, then Mrs Potter spoke with forced heartiness. 'Yes, miss, I'm sure you're right. We will send for Dr Smith. He was doctor to the old master, miss, and he will know what to do.' A glance of mutual understanding passed among the four family servants.

'I'll ride out and fetch him now,' Will said. 'Is that all right, miss?'

Deborah was too busy preparing the tea to notice that the servants were instinctively turning to her for their orders. 'Yes, thank you, Will,' she said. 'I shall sit with Lord Rutherford until the doctor comes.'

She waited impatiently for the doctor's arrival, her impatience made worse by the fact that she felt obliged to conceal it from Lord Rutherford. He lay quietly against the pillows, and his refusal to acknowledge the extent of his pain worried Deborah more than she cared to admit. She was very relieved when one of the young maids ran upstairs to announce that Will and the doctor had ridden into the yard.

She hurried downstairs and introduced herself to Dr Smith. He was a man of more than middle age, but he radiated energy and impressed her with his air of competence. He greeted Deborah politely, and asked briskly to be taken to see his patient.

It was more than half an hour before he returned to the drawing-room to deliver his verdict. 'You may stop pacing the floor, Miss Phipps,' he said with a kindly smile. 'Lord Rutherford says he has suffered from these sick headaches since he was a young man. Probably the strain of his father's illness contributed to the first attack, and I have told him that he makes himself more susceptible to these bouts by worrying. The muscles in his neck, Miss Phipps, were knotted with tension. Perhaps one of the servants can massage the affected area and thus reduce the pain. I can offer no other suggestions, except to tell you what I told Lord Rutherford. The pain will pass eventually, and it will pass sooner if he stops imagining that he suffers from the same affliction as his father.'

'Yes, I understand,' said Deborah, who in fact understood very little. 'Lord Rutherford's illness . . .' she murmured. 'I mean, the previous Lord Rutherford . . . The symptoms were not the same?'

The doctor's keen eyes examined her flushed cheeks. 'You need have no worries on that score, Miss Phipps. The late Lord Rutherford didn't have a headache until a few weeks before his death. His symptoms were entirely different and started with a slurring of his speech, followed by a gradual loss of vision. The late Lord Rutherford's symptoms were typical of his condition and the present Lord Rutherford shows none of them.'

Deborah managed a smile. 'Well, that is good news,' she said, hoping that was the proper thing to say. 'May I offer you some refreshment before you leave? It is a cold morning to set out without some hot tea or coffee to warm you.'

'Thank you, but I must be on my way. The squire became a grandfather for the first time last night, and I believe he may need some assistance this morning. He spent a fair part of the night celebrating and now he's paying the price—not to mention the rest of his long-suffering household!'

Deborah couldn't resist returning the doctor's smile. She followed his brisk progress into the hall, and welcomed his firm handshake. 'It's good to see this old cottage looking cared for again,' he said. 'Now, Miss Phipps, you remember to tell his lordship that the best thing he can do is to stop worrying about these occasional headaches of his. They're painful, but not the end of the world. And tell him not to pay any attention to the Dowager. I explained matters to the Dowager Lady Rutherford a dozen times, but I don't believe she ever understood what I was saying to her. And I've no doubt she passed on all her own confusions to her son.'

He clapped his hat firmly on his head and wrapped a long woven muffler several times around his throat. 'Goodbye, Miss Phipps. I shall

leave his lordship's health in your capable hands.
I am very glad you have come to take care of
him.'

CHAPTER
SIX

LORD RUTHERFORD was sufficiently recovered that evening to eat a light meal in his room. The next day, he insisted he was completely well again. His mood at breakfast seemed surprisingly cheerful, and Deborah decided that she need delay no longer in finding out the precise nature of her duties.

'My lord,' she said, as soon as the servants had left the breakfast-room. 'May I speak to you about the terms of my employment?'

'If you must. I was about to make a call on the bailiff.'

'I will detain you only a few minutes, my lord. I must know exactly what my job is. You have agreed to pay me a pound a week, but so far I have done nothing to earn such a generous wage.'

'Hinsdale Cottage has been transformed from top to bottom. And yet you consider that you have done nothing?'

'Well, very little. I merely helped the other servants to organise their routine more efficiently, but they have done all the hard work, my lord. Jenkins and Mrs Potter are eager for advice, and the two village girls will be excellent maids once they are properly trained.'

'How cosily domesticated you sound, my dear Miss Phipps.'

She flushed. 'I am sorry if you think I am encroaching. The training of your other servants is, of course, none of my business.'

'That's as may be,' Lord Rutherford muttered. It was some time before he spoke again. 'You are right about one thing, Miss Phipps. It is time I told you what I want you to do for me. There is no point in further delay. Come into the drawing-room and I will tell you why I brought you to Hinsdale Cottage.'

She followed him across the hall and saw that Jenkins had lit a fire in the drawing-room grate, but the room still smelled of mildew and the lingering dampness of long disuse. Lord Rutherford stood in front of the fire, staring into its depths. He did not ask her to sit down, nor did he preface his words with any opening pleasantries.

'When I found you on the pavement outside my town house, Miss Phipps, it occurred to me that you might possibly solve a problem which I have recently found increasingly troublesome. I brought you here because I wished to be alone with you, away from my family and friends, in order to observe your behaviour. I have spent the past few days considering your qualifications, Miss Phipps, and I have concluded you would do well for the job I have in mind.'

'Why, thank you, my lord. I'm very glad that I have pleased you.'

'You have not *pleased* me,' he said harshly. 'You have merely passed several elementary but essential tests. I don't know where or how you have acquired your knowledge, but I do believe you would be able to pass for a lady in almost any company. Your speech is without fault. Your table manners are excellent. You know how to carry on a polite conversation. You seem capable of organising a household. In short, Miss Phipps, I am urgently in need of a wife, and I have decided to offer you the position. It would be convenient if we could marry within the next few days.'

For several moments, Deborah did not move. Anger at his insulting categorisation of her accomplishments gave way to stunned disbelief. She eventually opened her mouth to speak, but no words came out. She took a deep breath and tried again, but her voice emerged only as an inelegant squeak. 'D-did you say . . . You can't have said that you want to marry me?'

'No,' he said. 'Of course I do not *want* to marry you. But I require a wife and I have decided you will fulfil the role as well as anyone I can hope to find.'

Deborah recovered her wits sufficiently to realise that Lord Rutherford's proposal was even less conventional and even less flattering than she had first thought. 'I do not understand what you are proposing,' she said, astonished at the false calm she succeeded in injecting into her voice. 'You say that you don't wish to marry me, but that you want a wife . . .'

'I am well satisfied with my bachelor state,' he responded curtly. 'There are reasons, however, both financial and social, why it has become apparent to me that I ought to marry.'

Deborah began to edge quietly towards the door. Although Lord Rutherford did not appear to be drunk, she was forced to conclude that he was deeply in his cups. Noblemen who were sober did not propose marriage to a woman who would have counted herself fortunate to be offered a job in his kitchens. She had had little experience with drunk-ards, but she was anxious to escape before Lord Rutherford's present mood of spurious rationality changed to violence. 'My lord,' she said placat-ingly. 'I think you are jesting, but I cannot see the point of your joke. I shouldn't have harassed you about the terms of my employment, I see that now. M-may I please have your permission to retire?'

He swung round to face her, his expression more grim than she had previously seen it. 'I am neither drunk nor otherwise out of my senses, Miss Phipps. I need a wife and I am offering you the job. Do you wish to take it or not?'

She pressed her hands to her flushed cheeks, still not quite able to believe the evidence of her own ears. 'You . . . you are really serious in this offer, are you not?'

'Eminently serious, Miss Phipps. And I should therefore be obliged if you would give me your reply.'

'You have said there are financial and social reasons why you ought to marry and I can under-stand that you may not wish to marry for love,' Deborah said, doing her best to sound calm and reasonable. (Could he possibly be sober? If so, could he possibly be sane?) 'But there must be many débutantes who would be honoured to become Lady Rutherford. Why could you not propose to one of them?'

Lord Rutherford walked across the room and helped himself to some brandy. He swirled the cognac in his glass for a moment before replying. 'I shall be honest with you, Miss Phipps. I don't wish for a conventional marriage in any sense of the word. I do not wish for a family and I do not wish for female companionship. In other words, I am offering a marriage which is formality only. I have no intention of changing my lifestyle to suit the pleasures of my wife. I offer no love, I cannot even offer affection. I shall be frank with you and say that I do not intend to consummate the marriage. My wife, therefore, will not be able to look forward to the pleasure of having her own children to care for and to love. In the circumstances, you will understand that I have little to offer this season's crop of eligible débutantes.'

She forced herself to meet his hooded gaze. 'Even so, my lord, I must ask why you have chosen *me*. You discovered me on your front doorstep and it is no secret that I was destitute. You know almost nothing about me, or my family background. How can you, the heir to a great family name, contemplate marriage to such a woman?'

'I have already explained that you will never be the mother of my children, Miss Phipps, so your family background is of little interest to me. I care only that your appearance and manners should not shame me if I am forced to introduce you to any of my friends. And, from your point of view, since you

admit you were destitute when I found you, I fail to
see why you hesitate to accept my proposal. It is my
intention that you should live here at Hinsdale
Cottage, and I shall provide you with an income
that is sufficient to maintain the household in considerable comfort. Since I am actively involved
with my work in the House of Lords, I spend the
majority of my time in London. I also have a family
estate in Somerset which must be cared for. You
will not, therefore, have to tolerate my company
except on rare occasions. I am guaranteeing you a
lifetime of comfort and financial security. Why do
you hesitate to accept? Surely my offer is a wonderful way for you to escape a future of endless hard
work and privation.'

'I am not frightened of hard work, my lord.'

'Perhaps not. But if you are not even a little
frightened at the prospect of a lifetime spent on the
edge of destitution, then you are a fool. And I had
not thought you to be a fool.'

'No, my lord, I believe I am not foolish. And
therefore I wonder why a great nobleman should
wish to enter into a marriage that is no real marriage at all. Why take a wife if you do not wish to see
her? Why burden yourself with her support if you
do not wish . . . that is, if you do not wish for an
heir.'

He looked at her coldly. 'I believe my reasons for
marrying are my own affair, Miss Phipps. You do
not need to understand my motives in order to
know that it is better to live at Hinsdale Cottage,
with an adequate income and the protection of my
name, than to spend your days wandering the

streets of London, uncertain of how you are to pay for your next meal. I see no cause for your hesitation.'

'Do you not? Perhaps I am overwhelmed by your generosity.'

He ignored her sarcasm. 'I will ask my lawyer to draw up papers that will ensure you financial security for the rest of your life, regardless of what might happen to me.'

'Happen to you, my lord? What could happen?'

He turned away, and his voice sounded impatient when he spoke again. 'It was a figure of speech, Miss Phipps. No more.'

Deborah was silent, unable to bring herself to reply, although she scarcely knew herself why she continued to demur. As Lord Rutherford himself had pointed out, what did she have to lose? His clipped words broke into the chaos of her thoughts.

'Perhaps, Miss Phipps, you would be good enough to favour me with a response to my proposal.'

'I don't know what to say,' she blurted out. 'It is not as easy as you pretend to reach so momentous a decision in the space of a couple of minutes. My lord, we know nothing about each other! How do I know that you are really Lord Rutherford? For all I know to the contrary, you may be an impostor, intent on some nefarious scheme. How do I know you are not a murderer? Or a madman? Heaven knows, your method of choosing a bride does not seem one that would be contemplated by a normal, law-abiding citizen.'

His hands tightened so fiercely round his glass of

cognac that Deborah thought the crystal stem might snap. He made no immediate reply to her outburst and, as the strained silence stretched out between them, she began to think he was going to withdraw his offer. When he finally answered her, his voice was low and flat, as though the effort of eliminating all emotion from his expression was almost too much for him to sustain.

'I shall repeat what I have already told you, Miss Phipps, I do not intend to spend time with my wife, nor do I intend to consummate the marriage. It is therefore incumbent upon me to choose a wife whose prospects of future happiness will not be blighted by those intentions of mine. If you are honest, you will acknowledge that you had no prospects at all when I found you, unless we consider the prospect of imminent starvation a desirable one. Therefore my behaviour, however unconventional, cannot detract from your prospects of future happiness. Had it not been for my intervention, you would probably have had no future.'

'I have already told you how grateful I am for your help.'

He ignored her whispered comment. 'As for your doubts about my identity, I shall introduce you to the vicar of the local church, who has known me since I was a small boy. He will be prepared to vouch for the fact that I am John Deveraux Rutherford, fifth baron, and a substantial landowner in Somerset. Do these reassurances satisfy you? If so, may I now be favoured with your answer?'

She looked once, quickly, at the arrogant line of his profile, then she stared at the floor. 'Yes, my lord,' she said huskily. 'I accept your offer.'

There was an almost imperceptible softening of the rigid line of his shoulders. 'In that case, Miss Phipps, I shall procure a special licence from the Bishop of Bath. And Mr Deake, the vicar I mentioned, will be able to marry us within the week.'

'I s-suppose you would not consider delaying the ceremony until we know one another a little better?'

'No,' he said ruthlessly. 'I would not consider it. I don't wish you to hold any illusions about this marriage, Miss Phipps. I neither wish nor intend for us to strive for a friendship which must, in the nature of things, be impossible. There is no reason for delay, and no point in it.'

'I am very sorry,' she said tartly. 'It was presumptuous of me to expect you to waste a whole week of your time in getting to know me. I apologise for forgetting, in the turmoil of the moment, that I am merely an insignificant scrap of humanity picked up from your doorstep. Whereas you, of course, are a great nobleman and therefore a perfect gentleman, always full of consideration for others.'

His mouth relaxed into the faintest hint of a smile. 'My manners may have been abrupt, Miss Phipps, and less than gentlemanly, but I have tried to be completely honest about the life you will lead after we are married.'

'Then I suppose I must be grateful to you for your honesty.' She covered her eyes with her hand, feeling a momentary panic at the realisation of

exactly what she had done. Marriage was an irre-
vocable step, and she wondered at the strange
twists in her moral values which permitted her
to wed Lord Rutherford, about whom she knew
nothing, when it had seemed intolerable to marry
Cousin George, whom she knew as a pillar of
respectability in his local community.

'Well, Miss Phipps, if you have finished frowning, shall we shake hands on our agreement?'

Tentatively she stretched out her hand, and he
took it in his grasp. His touch was cool and strong,
but for some reason her body felt hot and strangely
weak as his fingers curled around hers. She was
relieved when he abruptly released her and strode
across the room to the door. 'I intend to see at once
about our wedding arrangements,' he said. 'I shall
leave for Bath before lunch and ask the vicar to call
on you tomorrow, while I am gone.'

He left the room as she was still searching for
something suitable to say. The door shut noise-
lessly behind him. She listened to the sound of his
retreating footsteps until she could no longer hear
even the faintest echo. Silence descended upon the
drawing-room and she was left alone with nothing
to do save reflect upon the strangeness of Lord
Rutherford's proposal and the magnitude of her
folly in accepting it.

Three days later, Lord Rutherford returned from
Bath and announced that the marriage ceremony
would take place at eleven o'clock the following
morning at All Saints, which was the local parish
church. Deborah, whose habitual commonsense

had reasserted itself during his absence, attempted to protest.

'My lord,' she murmured, doing her best to sound firm and in command of the situation. 'We both acted hastily the other day. Of course we cannot be married. The idea is absurd.'

Her firmness had no effect upon Lord Rutherford. 'It is too late to change your mind,' he said curtly. 'The arrangements have been made and I already have the special licence. The vicar will be expecting us tomorrow morning. Did he not call on you yesterday?'

'Oh yes,' Deborah said. 'He was most courteous.'

'Then you can have no logical objections,' he said. 'You now have his word for it that I am indeed John Deveraux Rutherford, just as I claimed. There is nothing more to be discussed, so I will bid you good evening, Miss Phipps. Please be sure that you are ready to leave the house at half past ten in the morning.'

Deborah awoke to a bright, sunny day that mocked the dismal anxiety of her mood. She had not told the servants of her forthcoming marriage, since she could not quite believe in it herself, but her preparations for the ceremony were perforce so simple that she required no special assistance.

It had apparently not occurred to Lord Rutherford that his bride-to-be might need a new dress for the wedding. He had, in fact, returned from Bath without offering her so much as a length of ribbon or a bunch of roses to trim her bonnet. She was therefore obliged to wear the brown brushed wool dress she had worn every night for dinner, accompanied by the sturdy boots originally purchased by his housekeeper. Her wedding ensemble was topped off by her brown straw bonnet, which didn't quite match her dress, and her grey wollen gloves which, unfortunately, didn't quite match anything.

She had bathed and washed her hair the night before, and her clothes were so easy to slip into that she had no problem in descending punctually to the hall. Lord Rutherford was not yet there and as she paced the floor she happened to catch sight of herself in the cloakroom mirror. She found her reflected image entirely depressing. She looked more like a worn-out governess than a young woman on the way to her wedding.

Her gloomy mood was in no way lightened by the arrival of Lord Rutherford. Impeccably clad in a formal morning suit and spotless white linen, he looked so magnificent that Deborah's tiny store of confidence immediately dwindled to nothing. If she had secretly hoped that he might in some way alleviate her fears, such hopes were quickly dashed. He did not comment on her appearance—indeed, he scarcely glanced at her. He did not offer her a bouquet of roses to carry. He did not raise her hand to his lips and gallantly kiss it. He merely said, 'Good. You are on time,' and placed his hand impersonally beneath her elbow in order to escort her to the waiting carriage.

'I rented a small brougham in Bath,' he said as she settled herself inside the coach. 'There is nothing in the Hinsdale Cottage stables save a pony-trap and a gig, and neither looked safe enough to drive in. I shall see that they are both repaired before I return to London. You will want to have some means of getting about the country-side.'

'You are so thoughtful, my lord,' she said.

For the first time that morning he actually looked at her. 'I detect a note of sarcasm, Miss Phipps. Might I know what I have done to merit it?'

'Nothing,' she said tightly, furious with him and with herself. What did it matter if Lord Rutherford had found time to worry about his carriages, but had apparently still not realised that his bride was arriving at the church in an outfit more suited to a schoolroom than a wedding ceremony?

For a brief moment, the harshness of his expression softened. 'Don't be nervous, Miss Phipps. I promise you I will see to it that you never regret this morning's happenings.'

Perversely, now that he showed her kindness, she wished that he had not. It was somehow easier to accept what she was doing if her emotions were all sealed into a tight ball of anger. She turned away from the hint of warmth in his eyes. 'I can see no possible cause for regret,' she asserted, 'provided I am well paid.'

The warmth of his expression vanished instantly. 'I have told you that I shall see to your financial security,' he said, and looked silently out of the window for the remainder of their brief journey.

The vicar was a plump, elderly man of cheerful aspect and limited intellect. He greeted Lord Rutherford effusively, and bowed low over

Deborah's woollen-gloved hand. He could not disguise the fact that he was overwhelmed with curiosity about his patron's extraordinary choice of bride, but he conducted the wedding service with suitable dignity, his voice echoing hollowly in a church that was empty save for the bride and groom and two vicarage servants brought in as witnesses to the ceremony. When the register was safely signed, he wished the newly-weds lifelong happiness in a voice so patently full of doubt that Deborah was overcome by a nervous impulse to giggle.

Lord Rutherford showed no similar inclination to smile. He politely refused the vicar's offer of refreshment and quickly escorted Deborah to the waiting brougham. He ordered Will to drive back to Hinsdale Cottage with all possible speed and said nothing further until the carriage turned in through the iron gates at the end of the cottage driveway. 'I am going to summon the servants,' he said, 'I shall inform them of what has just taken place.'

Deborah could not contain a faint gasp of dismay. Telling the servants invested the ridiculous marriage service with a reality that had previously been lacking. 'Do they have to know?' she asked wretchedly.

'Of course they must know,' Lord Rutherford replied sharply as he assisted her from the carriage. They walked into the cottage arm in arm, and Deborah found that her legs were suddenly shaking. She turned to him, her hands tightening about his wrist in a panic-stricken grasp. 'We cannot do this!' she said to him through lips stiffened by fright. 'My lord, we have made a terrible mistake! We must go and tell the vicar to scratch our names from the register. We should never have married!'

'I'm afraid, my dear, that your second thoughts come about an hour too late. Surely it is not so terrible to face a few servants when you have already endured an entire wedding service without so much as a tremor?'

She bit her lip to stop it from trembling. 'Somehow it is much worse. The servants are real people, you see. But you are quite right, of course. There is nothing we can do now.'

Once again there was an infinitesimal softening of his manner. 'Take heart, my dear. It will not be so bad, I promise you.'

Jenkins was waiting in the hall. 'Tell the servants to come into the drawing-room,' Lord Rutherford said as he handed over his hat and cane. 'And, Jenkins, please bring a bottle of Madeira and eight glasses.'

He escorted Deborah into the drawing-room and she took off her bonnet, smoothing her hair nervously as they waited for the servants to arrive. When all six of them were gathered just inside the doorway, Lord Rutherford put out his hand and drew Deborah to his side. He smiled at her with such apparent tenderness that, if she had not known better, she would have believed him to be the most contented new husband in the world.

'I am happy to announce that this morning Miss Phipps and I were united in marriage by Mr Deake, the vicar of All Saints church. I know you will wish to offer the new Lady Rutherford your good wishes for her future happiness. Jenkins, the Madeira, if you please.'

The servants were clearly astonished, but by comparison with the vicar, their surprise seemed relatively muted. They accepted their glasses of the sweet wine with pleased smiles, and drank cheerfully when Jenkins proposed a toast to the long life and lasting happiness of the master and mistress. Then, one by one, they came up to Deborah and curtsied as they offered a renewal of their good wishes. She did not dare to meet their eyes when they addressed her as 'my lady'. She had not realised until this moment that, along with her marriage certificate, she had acquired a title. *Lady Rutherford*. The idea that she was now a baroness seemed too preposterous to treat seriously. Only a few days earlier she had been on the brink of starvation. The marriage ceremony once again took on the hazy outline of an event with little grounding in reality. She was relieved when the housekeeper hustled the servants away, saying that she would soon serve luncheon. At least the prospect of eating a meal seemed pleasantly normal.

When the servants had gone, Lord Rutherford turned to her. No trace remained of his earlier smiles. 'Well,' he said briskly. 'I trust you did not find that too difficult a task.'

'No, my lord.'

He looked at her averted face, and a flicker of emotion darkened his gaze. It was quickly doused. 'You have only to endure my company for a little longer,' he said. 'I shall be riding into Cheltenham this afternoon.'

'Very good, my lord. Does that mean . . . Am I permitted to spend the afternoon as I please?'

'You are Lady Rutherford now,' he said, and his voice had a cynical ring to it. 'You are my wife. Naturally, you may spend the afternoon as you see fit.'

She looked at him at last, her chin raised in a defiant tilt. 'We both know that is a lie, my lord. In every way that matters I am your servant, and obliged to seek your approval for the plans I make.'

'You have misinterpreted your role,' he said softly. 'Let it be understood, Lady Rutherford, that I have no interest in how you spend your days, provided your pursuits reflect no discredit upon my name. You are free to occupy yourself in any way that amuses you.'

A sudden coldness chilled Deborah's heart, but she was saved the necessity of finding a reply because Jenkins chose that moment to announce that luncheon was served.

Lord Rutherford offered his arm to Deborah with an ironic inclination of his head. She placed her icy hand on his sleeve, wondering if the butler had noticed the subtle mockery implicit in his master's bow. 'My dear,' Lord Rutherford said with exaggerated courtesy. 'I am sure you must be hungry. Shall we go in?'

CHAPTER
SEVEN

WHATEVER Lord Rutherford's true feelings about his new wife, and however much Deborah regretted her agreement to marry him, in the eyes of the servants she and Lord Rutherford were now a couple and they were treated as such. Lord Rutherford was expected to spend his evenings in the drawing-room with his bride, and Deborah was accorded all the respect due to a lady of the manor. The servants, far from resenting her new position, deferred to her wishes with a humble eagerness she found both absurd and touching. It was odd, Deborah reflected, how a simple fifteen-minute ceremony could effect such a profound change in her position.

To her relief, Lord Rutherford no longer subjected her to a constant scrutiny during their meals and his air of mockery seemed to have disappeared. She concluded that, having taken the decision to marry her, he was determined to make the best of it.

Despite his new forbearance, however, she discovered that a strange tension developed whenever they found themselves alone together. She could not fathom a cause for it, and eventually, for want of a better solution, ascribed it to her imagination. In any case, the sensation was not altogether unpleasant, and the time she spent with her husband after dinner was fast becoming the high point of her day.

They had been married for three days when the spell of fine weather came to an end. They were sitting together in the drawing-room after dinner when the storm finally broke in a resounding clap of thunder. Deborah sipped her coffee and listened to the pounding of the rain as it beat upon the slate roof. Fierce gusts of wind rattled the window-panes and the bare branches of the trees creaked in sympathy. She glanced at the leaping flames of the fire, giving a small sigh of contentment as she contrasted the cosiness of the drawing-room with the blustery darkness outside. She became aware of the fact that Lord Rutherford was watching her and she looked up to find him smiling, an expression she could not interpret shadowing his eyes.

'That was a very self-satisfied sigh,' he said.

She returned his smile somewhat shyly. It was moments like this that had kept her on edge ever since their marriage. 'I was just thinking how agreeable it is to hear the rain falling when we don't have to go outside. Everything in the cottage is so comfortable now! Even dinner tonight was quite well cooked. I do believe Mrs Potter has finally learned how to make pastry.'

'But not, unfortunately, how to boil vegetables.'

Risking another glance at him, she saw he was still smiling. 'We cannot expect miracles, my lord!'

'Why not?' Lord Rutherford enquired lazily. 'That is precisely what I have come to expect from you.'

She dropped her gaze to her lap, aware of a sudden leap of pleasure. 'I shall take that as a compliment, my lord.'

'A poor attempt at one. But come, tell me how you have occupied yourself today. What fabulous feats of organisation have you achieved while I've been plodding from field to field, discussing swedes and turnips and the benefits of enriching the soil with cow manure?'

She laughed, feeling a warm wave of happiness flow through her veins. 'We cleaned the library,' she replied. 'I think you will now find it a more comfortable place to work. Martha washed the windows, and the young maids and I removed the books from the shelves and dusted them all. We discovered a wonderful secret hidey-hole next to the fireplace and I expected to unearth a priceless family heirloom at the very least. Alas, the hole contained nothing more exciting than a pile of dust and a couple of dead spiders.'

'How frustrating for you! Did the books provide consolation? It is so long since I looked through the collection that I cannot remember what it contains.'

'There are a great many bound copies of sermons,' she said.

'Ah! You need say no more. I can see that the books were as disappointing as the secret hiding-place. Was there nothing of interest to make all your dusting worth while?'

'Oh yes, a few things. Some novels and a fascinating description of the Great Exhibition, with many fine drawings of the exhibits. I had no idea how many clever and useful things have been invented recently! Only think, somebody has manufactured a mangle efficient enough to remove the water from three bed-sheets at once, and with patented rubber rollers so that there is no danger of ripping the linen!'

'I share your amazement,' he said dryly. 'Was there nothing else apart from sermons and accounts of such mechanical marvels?'

'There were several travel books. There was a description of Lord Snow's journey into the Ottoman Empire, which was illustrated with some splendid photographs.'

'I should like to read it some time. I visited Greece with my tutor and we paid a brief visit to the city of Constantinople. I found it a fascinating place, although unbelievably dirty.'

'The book is over there, on the small table by the fire, if you would care to look at it.'

Lord Rutherford strolled across the room to pick up the book. He came and sat on the sofa next to Deborah, then began to leaf through the pages of Lord Snow's journal. 'The photographic work is certainly very fine,' he said. 'Did you see this picture of the Cathedral of Saint Sophia on the Bosporus? As you can see, it still looks more like a mosque than a place of Christian worship.'

As she turned to look at the photograph, Lord Rutherford leaned across to point out the minarets. Inevitably, his arm brushed the side of her breast, and a sharp stab of feeling immediately twisted through her. For a moment she was so shocked by the unexpected contact that she allowed her body to press against the hardness of his forearm. It was strangely exciting to feel his muscles curving into the softness of her breast, and her hand trembled as she held it out towards the book. For some reason it seemed difficult to breathe but, even so, she made no effort to move away from him.

He turned towards her and she saw that a startled expression darkened his eyes. She flushed scarlet with mortification and pulled away as though the touch of his arm had begun to burn her.

Lord Rutherford immediately stood up. 'I beg your pardon,' he said curtly. He dropped the book on a cushion at her side and walked quickly across the room. He helped himself to some brandy from the tray already set out by Jenkins and drank it in two or three hasty swallows. 'I have remembered that the bailiff left some accounts for me to examine,' he said. 'You will excuse me if I leave you. I bid you goodnight.'

'Yes,' she murmured, keeping her gaze carefully averted. The memory of the way she had pressed her body against his made her writhe with shame. 'Goodnight, my lord.'

His voice was low when he answered. 'Sleep well, Deborah.'

It was, she realised later, the first time he had ever called her by her first name.

The next morning, he left for London, informing her of his plans at breakfast-time, in the presence of the servants. There was nothing she could do except murmur polite wishes for a safe journey. When she asked how long he would be away, he replied that he didn't know. She managed to produce another smile as she expressed the formal hope that his business would go smoothly. Even if they had been alone, she could not have challenged his decision. He had warned her what to expect from her marriage, and she had no right to complain.

He caught the mid-day train, and the house seemed empty without him. She chivvied the servants into an orgy of cleaning and polishing, but at night, lying in her huge canopied bed, she found she had far too much time for thinking about how much she missed her husband's company. The knowledge that it might be weeks, even months, before she saw him again, caused a distinctly unpleasant feeling to settle somewhere in the pit of her stomach.

He returned on the Friday of the next week, bringing with him documents that set up the legal trusts providing for her future. A generous quarterly allowance took care of household expenses for Hinsdale Cottage, and he had even made provision for a personal income of five hundred pounds a year. Lord Rutherford took care to point out to her the clause which showed that these allowances were to be paid under 'all, any and every circumstance that might arise during her lifetime'. He seemed to find this clause of particular significance, but when she attempted to question him about it and to express her gratitude for the generous manner in which he had kept his side of their bargain, he waved away her thanks with noticeable irritation.

Her sense of obligation didn't blind her to the fact that her husband need not have travelled to London. His lawyers would have been more than willing to come to the cottage in order to assist such an important client. She wondered why he had chosen to leave her and go to London. Even more puzzling was the question why, having gone, had he decided to come back so quickly. Unfortunately she knew that this question, along with many others, was likely to remain unanswered.

In an effort to take her mind off the mysteries surrounding her new husband, Deborah began the task of repairing the household linen. She discovered that Mrs Potter was an excellent needlewoman, and each afternoon she and the housekeeper made themselves comfortable in the small ground-floor sitting-room where they darned their way through the piles of embroidered pillow-cases and monogrammed table-napkins. They had not yet even begun to tackle the cupboards full of towels and sheets, and Deborah thought wryly that she need never lack for useful occupation even if he left her alone for a year.

Mrs Potter was a naturally garrulous soul, and conversation flowed readily once she began to feel at ease with her new mistress. Guiltily, Deborah encouraged the housekeeper's gossip. She learned that the Dowager, Lord Rutherford's mother, lived permanently in London and had never visited Hinsdale since the death of her husband. Mrs

Potter hinted darkly that she hadn't paid many visits even when the poor old lord was alive. 'She doesn't go to Rutherford Place, neither, except at Christmas. She's a woman that can't abide the countryside, is the Dowager. 'Tis a good thing his lordship is wed. His people in Somerset need to have a mistress who takes an interest in the estate. I expect you'll be going there at Christmas, my lady. We shall miss you.'

There was nothing Deborah could say in the face of such remarks. Commonsense suggested the wisdom of cutting short the flow of confidences. Curiosity made such wisdom impossible. With ever-increasing interest and equally increasing guilt, she encouraged the housekeeper to chatter. Mrs Potter had assisted at the birth of Lord Rutherford and had immediately been hired as his nurse, so she possessed a fund of stories about her master's infancy and early childhood. According to her, no sweeter, kinder or more intelligent child had ever been born. 'Always chuckling, he was, and never a cross word to anybody. Ah, he was a little angel, the young master.'

At such moments, Deborah was forced to bite her tongue in order to avoid asking why this sweet, kind child had grown up into an aloof, arrogant man who almost never smiled and had not laughed in the entire month Deborah had known him. As far as she could see, only his superior intelligence had survived the transition from boy to man.

Inevitably, Deborah's curiosity finally overcame the last remnant of her discretion. Mrs Potter was in full flood, describing Lord Rutherford's first venture into the hunting field (naturally he had outrun most of the other riders). The housekeeper smiled fondly as she recalled the triumphant return of the old lord and his son, the fox's brush affixed to the young master's saddle, riders and mounts worn out from a bruising run across challenging countryside. 'That was one of the last times the old lord ever rode out,' she said. 'And I do believe it was the very last time the poor young master was ever completely happy. After that, he had to bear one burden after another, and no help from his mother. The poor little lad was probably happier when he was at school. I remember the expression on his face when he came home at Christmas and saw his father stumbling down the stairs, and his mother refusing to be in the same room . . .' The housekeeper stopped abruptly. 'This napkin's nothing but a mass of holes, my lady. Shall I throw it into the rag-bag?'

'Yes, do that,' Deborah replied hurriedly. 'Er . . . did the previous Lord Rutherford often . . . stumble? Is that why he retired to Hinsdale Cottage?'

'That and the rages,' Mrs Potter said, after a slight pause. 'It got so's he couldn't control them, and he worried that he might do somebody an injury. Of course, he never did. A wonderful man the old lord was, when he was himself, and I swear his real nature never changed right up to the end.'

Curiosity, guilt and a touch of horror all churned inside Deborah's head. She was far too absorbed in the housekeeper's story to hear the faint click of the door opening. 'The previous Lord Rutherford,' she prompted gently. 'Did he . . . did he drink excessive amounts of alcohol? Was that the reason for his bad temper?'

'Oh no, my lady . . .'

'I believe, Mrs Potter, that your presence is urgently required in the kitchen.'

Deborah looked up to see her husband framed in the doorway, and her cheeks were immediately stained with a dark flush of guilt. Mrs Potter gave a tiny gasp and scurried quickly from the room, pausing only to bob a frightened curtsy in the direction of her master.

Lord Rutherford strode into the room and Deborah felt a moment of true fear. His face was white with rage, his lips drawn into a twisted line of suppressed fury. A vein throbbed in his temple, heightening the impression of barely-restrained violence.

'It should not be necessary for me to say this,' he said, and his voice was so cold that Deborah literally shivered. 'But I shall make my orders explicit and then I do not expect them to be disobeyed—ever. You are not allowed, madam, to question the servants concerning matters that are in the past. Confine your intercourse with the staff to instructions concerning domestic matters.'

Deborah stood up, glad that her skirts covered the shakiness of her knees. 'I should not have gossiped with the housekeeper,' she said. 'I can only beg your pardon.'

'We will not speak of it any more.' Lord Rutherford prepared to leave the room.

'My lord . . .'

He stopped at the sound of her voice, but did not turn round to look at her.

'My lord, I am . . . I am your wife. Am I not entitled to learn anything about you or your family?'

He turned as she finished speaking, and his glance flicked over her, icy in its contempt. 'We both know you are not my wife in any true sense of the word,' he said brutally. 'You are my retainer, entitled to claim the title of spouse only by virtue of a trumpery piece of paper. We share nothing: no interests, no heritage, no shred of affection. It is time you understood, madam, that you have no entitlements unless I care to give them to you.'

He closed the door quietly behind him, his rigid control more frightening than any outburst of fury could possibly have been. Deborah sank back into the chair. The fire still blazed in the hearth, the autumn sunlight still gleamed through the shining window-panes, but she felt a chill so severe that she wondered if her body would ever feel warm again.

She had dreaded facing Lord Rutherford across the dinner-table that evening, but she discovered that there was a great deal to be said for the discipline instilled by years of living in Cousin George's conventional household. She was a little late coming downstairs, but she forced herself to take her accustomed place opposite her husband. He, in turn, greeted her with evident restraint but nevertheless with formal courtesy. Deborah did her best to pretend she was eating, and the dreadful meal finally came to an end.

She had every intention of escaping to her bedroom as soon as they left the dining-room, but Lord Rutherford's low voice halted her at the foot of the stairs. 'Would you be good enough to come into the drawing-room? I have something to discuss with you.'

She had no choice but to obey. She followed him across the hall and waited, reluctantly, just inside the drawing-room door.

Lord Rutherford stood by the fire, one hand resting on the mantelpiece and one foot on the gleaming brass fender. His stance should have suggested a man at ease with the world, but Deborah saw that his other hand was clenched into a tight fist at his side and his face, in so far as she could see it, seemed weighted with care. He turned to her at last. 'I wish to apologise,' he said with extreme formality. 'My behaviour this afternoon was—inappropriate to the magnitude of your indiscretion. I do not wish you to gossip with the servants, but my manner . . . my manner in reproving you was excessively harsh.'

The chill which had gripped Deborah slowly relaxed its grasp. She found herself struggling against an incomprehensible urge to smooth away the deep lines of anxiety marking Lord Rutherford's face. She wondered what it would feel like to raise her hand and run it along the rigid outline of his jaw. She pressed her hand to her eyes, wiping away the inappropriate images.

'You spoke only the truth, my lord,' she said in a

low voice. 'I am a servant whom you have hired to perform a specific task. I accepted the job, so I am obliged to follow your wishes as to how that job should be performed. We are neither of us at ease in this strange marriage, but I still would like to believe that one day we may be able to think of each other as friends.' She looked down at her fingers, which were twisted into a tight knot of tension. 'I already enjoy your companionship, my lord, and I hope . . . I hope that you are pleased with the way I am caring for Hinsdale Cottage.'

'How could I fail to appreciate the changes you have wrought?' His gaze returned to its previous contemplation of the fireplace. 'Deborah, I have decided that we are thrown too much into each other's company here at the cottage. The enforced intimacy . . . In short, I have decided that we should spend some time in London. I have made arrangements for us to leave tomorrow morning.'

'Tomorrow morning! You wish me to accompany you?'

'Yes. When I was in town I informed my mother of the fact that I had married, and a formal announcement appeared in the Court Circular over a week ago. Naturally, my mother wishes to meet you.'

Deborah gulped in a few nervous breaths, then walked further into the room so that she could hold the back of a chair for support. 'You h-have published an announcement about our wedding? In the newspapers?'

'You surely did not imagine that I would keep the

fact a secret? What would be the point in marrying you if I did not intend the world to know that I am wed?'

She was overcome by a sudden memory of that last, fateful conversation with her landlady, and the boast she had made concerning her mythical engagement to a non-existent nobleman. A superstitious tremor rippled along her spine. Was this to be the punishment for her lies? That they should come true, but in a way that denied her all hope of real happiness? She saw that Lord Rutherford was waiting for a reply, and she did her best to speak calmly although she felt more like screaming or bursting into hysterical laughter.

'I shall look forward to meeting the Dowager Lady Rutherford,' she said. For a second or so, Lord Rutherford's attention was fixed so closely upon her that she could not maintain her false composure and she blurted out the first question that came into her head. 'Does your mother know the truth about our marriage?' she asked.

'Not exactly,' he said, and it was so long before he said anything more that she knew he was debating precisely what he needed to tell her. 'She . . . my mother . . . believes it to be a normal marriage, contracted in much the usual way. I told her that your parents recently died and that you found yourself alone in the world. I suggested that our . . . feelings . . . were deeply involved with each other and we saw no reason to wait. I said that our wedding was kept private because you were still in mourning.' A dark wave of colour stained his cheekbones as he finished speaking, and she guessed that he hated to confess a lie—and a lie, moreover, of such a nature.

So, she thought, his mother is no more aware than I am of the true reasons why Lord Rutherford decided to contract a false marraige with a destitute bride. This insight brought her only momentary comfort, however, since she could foresee considerable difficulties with the story Lord Rutherford had chosen to concoct. 'I wish you had given your mother some other explanation of our hasty marriage,' she said. 'Surely it will be very difficult to convince the Dowager Lady Rutherford of the truth of your tale.'

'How so?'

'You have credited us with making a love match,' she said. 'According to your story, we are so passionately attracted to each other that we could not wait for a conventional period of mourning before marrying.'

'And so?' he enquired coldly.

She drew in a tiny breath. 'You do not behave like a man willing to count the world well lost for love, my lord.'

For a moment the coldness of his expression vanished into something quite different, but the icy indifference was in place again so quickly that she could not decide why or how she had shocked him. 'Does it bother you that I am not prepared to sing the praises of your beauty?' he asked with a hateful touch of mockery. 'Does it bother you that I don't spend the evenings whispering sweet nothings into your ear? Do you miss the attentions of your previous lovers more than you anticipated? You are forgetting, madam, that a gentleman's behaviour towards his wife bears no similarity to the way a man conducts himself when he is with his paramour. There is no reason for me to sigh and swoon over you just because I have told my mother we are in love. The Dowager Lady Rutherford is a noblewoman by birth, by marriage and by centuries of breeding. We are man and wife, so she will not expect any vulgar public displays of affection between us.'

'How fortunate that aristocratic behaviour is so hypocritical, because my skill at dissembling is certainly not equal to the task of pretending to like you, let alone to love you! Thank God your mother is so noble that I shall be spared the horror of having to participate in any *vulgar displays of affection*. If you have no further instructions for me, my lord, I bid you good evening.'

She turned to leave the room, her anger so great that she did not look where she was going. It occurred to her briefly that her anger was out of proportion to the tastelessness of his remarks. Why should Lord Rutherford's arrogance and lack of sensitivity cause a red mist of fury to swim before her eyes? She swirled round, and the sweep of her skirts knocked a china shepherdess from her perch on a small table by the door. The painted head parted from the pink-gowned body and lay, incongruously simpering, on the polished wooden floor.

She picked up the broken pieces, her anger still seething. 'I regret that I have broken this work of art,' she said. 'However, as my employer, you know that I am being excessively well paid for doing very little. You may deduct the cost of a replacement from my wages.'

'Put those wretched lumps of china down,' he said, and she was astonished to detect a note of wry amusement in his voice. 'You have no idea how angry you look, like one of the Greek Furies about to descend upon an unsuspecting mob of sinners. If I beg your pardon for my lack of courtesy, will you calm yourself and agree to listen to the plans I have made for your stay in London?'

She looked at him for several tense seconds then, silently, replaced the broken shepherdess on the table without moving from her position by the door.

'Do come a little closer to the fire,' he invited, 'so that I know I am forgiven.' She hesitated, and when she finally obeyed, his mouth curved into a smile of devastating charm. She stared determinedly at the floor so that she would not have to see how his face was warmed and softened by the glow of laughter reflected in his eyes. 'Thank you,' he said. 'It is difficult to talk over a fifteen-foot gap of outraged disapproval.'

She risked a brief glance in his direction. He was still smiling, so she quickly looked back to the embers of the fire. 'What did you want to say to me, my lord?'

'I wanted to say that you were right to claim that we are neither of us at ease in this strange marriage. We both have to struggle to find out how we must deal with one another and we have nobody to turn to for useful advice. I spoke thoughtlessly just now and I am sorry if I caused your feelings to be hurt. I did not really intend it to be so. Shall we shake hands to show that we are friends again?'

She held out her hand and felt her fingers enclosed in his firm grasp. For a moment, she was ridiculously tempted to move closer to him. She wanted to rest her head against the broad strength of his shoulders and to bask in the warmth of his unexpected kindness, but she did not succumb to the urge. She removed her hand and strove to keep all hint of emotion out of her voice when she answered him. 'Your apology is accepted, my lord. What did you wish me to know about our trip to London?'

'I wish only to reassure you of how easy you will find life there. I will not expect anything very difficult of you, I promise.'

'What precisely will you expect me to do?' she asked, aware of a renewed flash of anger. Did he still believe her so incompetent that she needed to be protected at every turn?

He misinterpreted the stiffness of her reply. 'I understand that you are frightened at the thought of being introduced into London society,' he said. 'It is very natural that you should feel overwhelmed by the prospect of meeting so many important people. However, you will in reality have little contact with any of my friends. Naturally, I won't expect you to entertain on my behalf and I will do my best to ensure that you are never put into a social situation that would embarrass you.'

'How good of you!'

He smiled reassuringly, unaware of her sarcasm.

'As you know, I want the world—*my* world—to accept that I am happily married. That is the sole purpose of our stay in town. But I anticipate no particular problems. I shall almost always be with you when you visit my mother, and we can arrange for you to be seen only in public places where there is limited opportunity for conversation.'

'Why not put about the story that I am deaf and dumb, my lord?'

For a moment his smile was replaced by a frown of concentration, and she realised to her horror that he was seriously considering her proposal. 'No,' he said finally. 'I do not think that would serve. I shall take you to the Opera, I think, and once or twice to Morning Service at some fashionable church.' Almost to himself, he added, 'I can make sure you are superbly, but modestly, dressed and my acquaintances will draw their own conclusions as to why I married you. Yes, the more I think of it, the more convinced I am that you need hardly say a word to anybody. God knows, half the débutantes in any season are incapable of saying two sensible words in succession. I see no reason why we should not be able to pull the thing off.' He flashed Deborah another charming smile. 'You see, it is as I promised you. You need not worry about anything. I shall ensure that you will be required to do nothing more difficult than to look beautiful. And just think of the pretty new dresses I shall ask my mother to buy for you!'

Deborah nearly bit off her tongue in a valiant effort not to tell Lord Rutherford just what he could do with his brilliant plans and his pretty little dresses. The memory of what it felt like to be homeless, penniless and hungry came to her rescue. Temper tantrums were a luxury she could not afford. Since leaving Cousin George's house she had learned the wisdom of not fighting battles a single minute before they were necessary.

She drew some comfort from the fact that, whether he realised it or not, Lord Rutherford had already altered the conditions laid down for their marriage. Only a few weeks previously he had insisted that she would never be allowed to accompany him to London. Now he was debating how best he could introduce her to his friends. She was certain, once they were in town, that she would find many more opportunities to change the terms of their marriage contract, but did not stop to ask herself why this had become so urgent. She merely pushed the confusing welter of thoughts to the back of her mind and concentrated on smiling her agreement to her husband's plans. Yes, she assured him, she would be ready to catch the early morning train to London and yes, she would go upstairs now to do her packing.

It was only when she was alone in her bedroom, neatly stacking her meagre pile of possessions into the old carpet-bag, that she had time to think, and then she couldn't resist a few glorious daydreams about the dresses he had promised her. In her mind's eye she saw herself, clad in a wonderful new ball-gown, dancing the night away in her husband's arms. She was so busy mentally bestowing blue bows and scattered white rosebuds over the loops of her crinoline that she scarcely noticed the most important part of her daydream, which was the rapt expression in Lord Rutherford's eyes as he looked down, smiling tenderly at his wife.

CHAPTER
EIGHT

As THEIR train pulled into Paddington station, Deborah realised she was about to return to the house where her acquaintance with Lord Rutherford first began. The servants who were at this moment preparing to welcome the new Lady Rutherford were the self-same ones who had seen a ragged and fish-scented Deborah locked into the boot-boy's abandoned bedroom. In such circumstances, the prospect of meeting her household staff was not a pleasant one.

She did her best to overcome her anxiety as she stepped on to the platform, but she was not encouraged by the reaction of Lord Rutherford's coachman. This worthy bowed deeply, then nearly toppled over his own feet when he straightened up and recognised exactly who his new mistress was. If there been any flies around so late in the year he would have caught several, for his mouth hung wide open and his eyes bulged with shock right up to the moment when Lord and Lady Rutherford were safely bestowed in the brougham and the door slammed shut behind them.

Deborah could not make up her mind whether to laugh or to cry. 'My lord,' she said as the coach jolted into motion. 'You saw how the coachman behaved. What on earth are we to do about the servants at Rutherford House? What are you going to tell them about me?'

'I shall tell them you are my wife,' he said. 'What other explanation is necessary?'

'Servants judge their own status by the social status of their masters,' Deborah pointed out. 'They no doubt expected you to marry the daughter of a duke, or at the very least the daughter of an earl. They will feel personally insulted when they realise that the Miss Deborah Phipps of the wedding announcement is not only a commoner, but the same tattered female who recently passed the night in one of their downstairs cubbyholes.'

He shrugged, refusing to see her difficulty. 'I have told you that you will have my support,' he said. 'I don't see that the opinions of my domestics are of any particular significance to either of us.'

She sighed, wishing that she shared just a touch of her husband's inborn arrogance. She glanced at him and saw that his face was somewhat pale and his hands were clenched tightly in his lap. Perhaps, she concluded, he is not quite as indifferent to the opinion of the servants as he would have me believe.

Their arrival at Rutherford House was every bit as difficult as Deborah had anticipated. The servants, wearing their best uniforms, were lined up to greet their master and his bride. Several of the younger maids were so startled to recognise who this new bride actually was that they forgot to curtsy as she and her husband performed the obligatory ritual walk down the full length of their assembled ranks.

Lord Rutherford earned her deep gratitude by treating her with superb, formal courtesy, tactfully ignoring the maids whose amazement overcame their training, and murmuring polite words of greeting to the servants who best managed to disguise their astonishment. He personally escorted her upstairs, and instructed the housekeeper to follow with hot water and a tray of refreshments. Her ladyship, he announced with a bland smile, was fatigued from the exertions of her journey.

Deborah followed Lord Rutherford into her bedroom, relieved that no servant had accompanied them. By comparison with the daunting ranks of servants, her husband seemed quite relaxing company. The master suite consisted of two bedrooms and two dressing-rooms connected by a shared sitting-room. Lord Rutherford remained courteous but impersonal as he pointed out the various conveniences of her rooms. 'I trust that you will be able to rest comfortably this afternoon,' he said as they completed their brief tour. 'I myself am planning to leave shortly for the House of Lords, but I suppose I ought to return in time to join you for dinner. The servants will expect us to dine together on our first night in town.'

She was aware of an irrational moment of regret because he so obviously wished to avoid her company. 'Oh,' she said airily. 'Who are we to concern ourselves with the expectations of the servants?'

He looked at her sharply before striding towards

the door of his bedroom. 'As you say. Nevertheless, I shall see you at dinner, madam.'

She saw that his shoulders were stiff with repressed anger and she was illogically pleased by this evidence of her power to disturb him. 'My lord!' She called him back before he could leave the room. 'I am not at all tired,' she said. 'In fact, I wish to go shopping this afternoon. Could you please tell me how I may draw on my allowance?'

He frowned. 'What do you wish to buy?'

'Oh, not too much,' she said. 'Only dresses, shoes, bonnets, a cloak, gloves, nightgowns, scarves, muffs, ribbons, lace, tippets . . .'

To her relief, he interrupted her list with a burst of genuine laughter. She couldn't remember ever seeing him laugh before and she thought how well the action became him. 'Enough!' he exclaimed. 'I take your point! I agree that you are in urgent need of some new clothes.' With a half-smile that for some reason turned her knees to water, he added, 'I don't think either of us shares my housekeeper's passion for the colour brown.'

'Then I may go shopping this afternoon?'

'Tomorrow,' he said after a pause. 'I shall send a message to my mother at once and we shall see if a shopping expedition can be arranged for tomorrow morning.'

'I should prefer to shop alone, my lord. It will be embarrassing for me—for both of us—if your mother meets me before I have had some chance to improve the extent and quality of my wardrobe.'

'There may be some degree of awkwardness,' Lord Rutherford admitted. 'But I am afraid that I cannot allow . . . It would not be suitable for you to go shopping alone.'

'Why not?' she asked, striving to speak calmly, although she knew only too well the reason for his prohibition. He didn't trust her to choose her new clothes wisely or tastefully.

'There are several good reasons,' he said stiffly. 'Ah, here is Mrs Bowler with your luncheon tray and a maid with some hot water. I shall leave you to rest now, my dear.' He inclined his head in a polite gesture of farewell and hurried from the sitting-room. The young maid followed him.

Deborah walked over to the heavily-curtained windows, drawing back the folds of Nottingham lace in an ostensible desire to look out at the view. In fact she needed a few moments to gather her resources so that she could face the housekeeper without revealing any of her inner trepidation. Mrs Bowler had not approved of her before, and was unlikely to feel any more warmly now. Deborah waited until she was quite sure she had her expression under control before she turned to greet the housekeeper. 'Thank you, Mrs Bowler,' she said. 'The tea will prove very welcome.'

'Yes, my lady.'

The faint note of scorn in the housekeeper's voice brought a flush of high colour to Deborah's cheeks. She was supremely conscious of the fact that she was still wearing an outfit that Mrs Bowler had chosen for her, and she was suddenly furious with Lord Rutherford that he should have brought her to London without providing her with a few clothes more fitting to her position as his wife. She

decided then and there that she would not tolerate
meeting his mother and having to endure the same
expression of disdain mingled with faint pity.

She walked over to the wash-stand and poured
hot water into the delicate porcelain washbowl. She
turned her back so that the housekeeper would not
see that her hands were shaking. 'I shall take fifteen
minutes to refresh myself,' she said. 'Then send all
the upstairs maids to me. I wish to appoint my
personal maid before I go shopping.'

'His lordship said that you were going to rest this
afternoon, my lady.'

Deborah dried her hands on a lace-edged linen
towel and turned to face the housekeeper. 'Lord
Rutherford over-estimated my fatigue,' she said,
and the thread of steel underlying her words was
clearly audible. 'I expect the maids in fifteen
minutes, Mrs Bowler.'

'Yes, my lady.'

Deborah finished washing away the grit and
grime of the train journey and enjoyed two cups of
tea. She was too excited to eat, and she wondered
how she had so quickly forgotten what it felt like to
be permanently hungry. She was once more standing by the window when Mrs Bowler returned with
the seven upstairs maids. Deborah selected one
called Margaret, simply because she looked friend-
lier than any of the others. She asked the housekeeper to summon the carriage and announced that
she was leaving for Bond Street. She and her new
maid were seated in the brougham almost before
she had time to question the wisdom of what she
was doing.

It was wonderful to walk into the bustling London shops, knowing that she had the incredible sum of one hundred and twenty-five pounds (her quarterly allowance) to spend on whatever she pleased. That she was deliberately defying Lord Rutherford's instructions added a spice to her actions. She was tempted to wander from store to store, admiring the elegance of the window displays and the breathtaking range of goods available for purchase, but she resisted, because she knew she was short of time. It was going to be difficult to find any suitable dresses, since most good quality clothing was, of course, made to order. She knew that even the big London stores, with their many different departments and their ultra-modern selling techniques, carried only models of ladies' gowns which were then made to the exact measurements of individual purchasers.

She decided not to worry about the problems of finding a dress until she had purchased some other necessities. She started by buying herself a new pair of walking-shoes and a plain white pair of evening slippers. She could scarcely contain an ecstatic grin as she and her maid left Mr Lobb's shoe shop. As she had anticipated, her lack of cash had proved no problem at all. A simple announcement of her identity, coupled with an instruction to send the bill to her husband's town house, was quite sufficient to ensure her instant, courteous attention.

Pleased with her easy success, she visited two more shops, where she acquired a pair of grey kid gloves, a grey straw bonnet trimmed with white grosgrain ribbons and pink rosebuds, and a grey tweed tippet with a velvet collar and pink silk lining. Margaret, still overawed by her sudden elevation to lady's maid, recovered her tongue sufficiently to express rapturous admiration of both the tippet and the bonnet, providing a welcome boost to Deborah's self-confidence.

At Swan and Edgar's she bought some lace-trimmed underwear and tried on the model for a woven wool afternoon dress. Succumbing to temptation, she also tried on the model for a simple cerulean blue silk evening-dress and, since this fitted her precisely, she concluded that Fate had obviously ordained that she purchase it.

Once again she had no difficulty in persuading the obsequious shop assistants to sell her the dresses. Her name and title, together with the vague hint that she might be returning to buy more in the future, were quite sufficient to ensure the immediate wrapping of both dresses into layers of tissue paper, and the despatch of the senior fitting-room attendant and a delivery-boy to carry the purchases to her carriage. No suggestion was made that she should wait two or three days while the Emporium's seamstresses ran up a copy for her.

Flushed with her triumphs, Deborah arrived back at Rutherford House in barely enough time to change before dinner. She bathed quickly, then stood quite still while Margaret helped her into the blue silk evening dress and fastened the row of tiny buttons that closed the back. As soon as the maid had adjusted the frills of the skirt, she turned up the gas-lamp. 'Look in the mirror, my lady,' she said. 'You were beautiful before, but now . . .'

Hesitantly, Deborah looked into the swinging cheval-glass. The classical beauty of her features stared back at her, enhanced by a complexion rendered more perfect then ever by three weeks of good food and fresh country air. The blue of her dress emphasised the dark azure glow of her eyes. The simple style displayed the slenderness of her waist, and the low neckline left her shoulders almost bare. In the glow of the gaslight, her reflection shimmered with a subtle aura of restless expectation that sharpened the edge of her beauty, heightening it to a new level of power. She turned away from the mirror, uncomfortable with what she saw there.

'Will that be all, my lady?' Margaret asked.

'Yes, yes, thank you. You may go.'

The maid reached the doorway and collided with Lord Rutherford, who burst in unannounced, waving a sheaf of papers in his hand. Margaret did not wait for fresh instructions. After one look at her master's face, she scuttled hastily away.

Lord Rutherford ignored the departure of the maid. He stormed over to confront Deborah, thrusting the papers under her nose. 'What is the meaning of this?' he roared and then fell suddenly, strangely, silent.

She looked up just in time to catch a glimpse of stunned admiration in his eyes before the familiar mask descended, cutting off all evidence of his true feelings. 'What is the meaning of what, my lord?' she asked softly. She took the papers from his unresisting fingers and glanced at them with feigned casualness. 'Why, my lord, these are bills.

They are accounts of my purchases sent to you from various London shops, my lord.'

'I am not a fool! I am perfectly well aware of the fact that they are bills.'

'I'm so sorry. I thought you asked me what they were and I simply tried to explain.'

Lord Rutherford ground his teeth. 'Let me express myself with painstaking clarity, madam. I wish to know why you spent the afternoon shopping, in express defiance of my wishes.'

Deborah lifted her head in a rebellious gesture. 'Your wishes were unreasonable,' she said. 'I didn't want to meet your mother dressed in clothes that displayed an excruciating lack of good taste. How can she possibly believe our marriage is a normal one when my wardrobe consisted of two brown dresses, both of dubious quality and even more dubious style?'

'I consider the beliefs of the Dowager Lady Rutherford concerning this marriage to be my affair—and mine alone.'

She sighed, curiously depressed by the bleakness of his manner. 'I'm sorry if I have offended you, my lord, but I did not enjoy being a laughing-stock for your servants. How did you expect me to take charge of your household when I had nothing to wear except garments that your own housekeeper had bought for me?' Her voice shook and she looked appealingly at her husband's averted profile. 'My lord, I am now your wife. It is insulting to you, as well as to me, if I am not allowed to dress in a manner which is suited to my role.'

'You have not been hired to question my decisions,' he said coldly. 'Your role, madam, is to obey me. That is the role of every woman once she is wed. Allow me to remind you of the vows you made during the wedding ceremony.'

'We both made many promises during that service which have not been fulfilled,' Deborah said, feeling a fresh spurt of anger. 'If *you* remember, my lord, you promised to love me and to cherish me. And I, in turn, promised to love you, as well as to obey your orders. Why am I supposed to remember one vow and not the other?'

There was a considerable pause. 'It is, of course, absurd to talk of love between the two of us,' he said. 'That is an entirely different matter.'

'Is it? I'm afraid I don't understand why one promise must be kept, while another may be ignored with impunity. And I completely fail to see why you want a wife whose clothing suggests that her position lies somewhere between an ill-trained governess and an upper housemaid.'

'I do not believe you could ever look like a governess,' he said. Abruptly he turned away from her. 'The damage has already been done. You have your new dresses, and lord knows what else besides, so it is pointless to pursue this conversation. I believe dinner is ready. Perhaps we should go down together.'

Courteously, Lord Rutherford stood to one side as she went through the door. With equally impersonal courtesy he offered his arm to support her down the sweeping staircase and into a diningroom resplendent with brilliant chandeliers and massed displays of table silver and flowers. The butler bowed as they entered. Three maids curtsied and two footmen pulled out their chairs. Deborah bit her lip in an effort to control a faintly hysterical gurgle of laughter. She glanced up, noticing that a wry smile hovered at Lord Rutherford's lips, and realised that this ostentatious display was not customary. Presumably, therefore, it was chiefly for her benefit. She wondered whether the splendour had been intended to impress her or to intimidate her. Either way, she decided, it would be wiser to pretend that she was delighted with the elaborate preparations.

'How very lovely the table looks,' she said as soon as she was seated. 'The floral arrangements are particularly attractive, don't you agree, my lord? Perhaps you happened to mention to the housekeeper that yellow chrysanthemums are my favourite autumn flower?'

Lord Rutherford shot her a brief glance in which admiration and surprise mingled equally. 'No, my dear. The choice of chrysanthemums must be accounted a happy accident. I did, however, mention to the cook that you are particularly fond of gooseberry tart, and she promised to prepare one of her very best.'

It was Deborah's turn to be astonished. 'H-how did you know my preference? I don't recall mentioning anything to you . . .'

He smiled again. 'Your habit of taking three helpings each time it was served at Hinsdale Cottage provided a useful clue, my dear.'

A becoming flush of pink rippled into her cheeks. 'Surely not *three* helpings,' she murmured.

'Besides, it was most ungallant of you to count.'

Lord Rutherford smiled, then took pity on her evident confusion and changed the subject. 'I conferred this afternoon with Mr Catterick, the Member of Parliament who is to introduce my Bill on factory legislation into the Commons. He believes it will come up early in the present session.'

Deborah was gratified that he chose to discuss his work with her, and she responded with interest. The undercurrent of tension disappeared completely as the topics of their conversation roamed and widened. The brown Windsor soup was replaced by grilled trout, and their conversation left the hazards of factory work and switched to the appalling state of labourers' cottages in urban Lancashire. With the arrival of the roast beef, Deborah suggested the possibility of legislation to prevent dishonest builders constructing cottages that failed to meet certain minimum standards of durability. Lord Rutherford considered her idea, pointing out all the difficulties of regulating an industry that involved so many trades and constantly moved its location.

The footmen and the maids exchanged disbelieving glances, and for once the butler was entirely in harmony with their unexpressed opinions. Whatever he had expected from this first dinner under a new mistress, it had not been an earnest discussion of cotton shortages caused by the American Civil War and methods of preventing jerry-building of low-cost housing. Despite the best efforts of the cook, neither the master nor the mistress seemed aware of what they were eating until the arrival of the gooseberry tart, when her ladyship suddenly looked across at his lordship with a shy smile. 'It was good of you to remember one of my favourite dishes, my lord. I—I am touched by your thoughtfulness.'

'It was my pleasure,' he said, and her smile became radiant as they looked into each other's eyes.

The new mistress had a smile that would melt the heart of a marble statue, the butler thought, and Lord Rutherford was no statue. The pie began to grow cold on their plates and the butler finally ventured a discreet cough. As a married man of some years' standing, he considered that there was no point in ruining a perfectly good dessert when you had the whole night ahead of you. At the sound of the butler's cough, Lord and Lady Rutherford hastily took up their spoons.

'The weather was very fine this afternoon,' Deborah said. 'We have been fortunate to see so much sunshine this late in October.'

'Yes, indeed. The farmers have been blessed this year. It rained when it was supposed to, and the sun came out for the hay-making and for the harvest. Naturally, the old-timers are full of grim predictions for the winter.'

'Naturally. And how disappointed they will be if the winter should turn out to be mild!'

They were off again, the butler thought. He'd never heard such a rum selection of subjects for a pair of newly-weds to discuss, particularly when the two of them were obviously head over heels in love. The air simply crackled every time one of them

happened to catch the other's eye. Mrs Bowler
had confided to him that she couldn't understand
how his lordship had come to marry a woman so far
beneath him in the social scale. The butler found it
no mystery at all. A man needed only one glance in
Lady Rutherford's direction to understand exactly
why Lord Rutherford had chosen her.

The newly-weds had finished eating, and the
butler signalled for the dishes to be cleared. He was
not surprised when Lord Rutherford waved away
the decanter of port. 'I shall ring later if we want
coffee,' he said.

He and Deborah walked upstairs, passing out of
the butler's sight as they chattered animatedly
about the sights of Rome. Lord Rutherford had
visited the city only once, but Deborah had been
there several times and he was interested in her
account of the archaeological excavations just
beginning in the ancient forum.

When they reached their private sitting-room,
she sat on the love-seat pulled close to the fire. Lord
Rutherford sat beside her, talking amusingly of his
youthful adventures in southern Europe. Little by
little, he persuaded her to recount some of her own
childhood experiences and she soon found herself
laughing with him at the happy memories her
stories evoked. She began to relax in his company
in a way that was both pleasurable and entirely new
to her. Sometimes it seemed as though she had only
to express half an idea before he understood the
whole. Time lost its meaning, and she was startled
when she glanced up at the little ormolu clock on
the mantel and saw that its hands were pointing to

midnight. She tried unsuccessfully to smother a yawn, suddenly aware of how sleepy she was.

'Have we talked too long?' Lord Rutherford asked, and for some reason his intent gaze brought a rush of colour to her face.

'I am a little tired. I hadn't realised it was so late.'

'Neither had I,' he said. I've enjoyed our conversation.'

Deborah was suddenly conscious of the fact that she and her husband were completely alone, seated intimately together on a small love-seat. His arm rested along the back of the chair and, if he moved it only a fraction of an inch, it would come to rest upon the bare slope of her shoulders. She gave an involuntary shiver as the velvet of his evening jacket brushed against her skin.

'Deborah . . .' he murmured. 'Are you cold?' His hand curved round her arm, pulling her gently towards him, and her heart immediately began to beat with a quick, erratic rhythm.

'I'm not cold,' she said. His fingers traced a delicate pattern over her shoulders, and breathing became so difficult that she wondered if her lungs had ceased functioning. She pulled away from his clasp and sprang up from the love-seat. 'It's time for me to go to bed,' she gasped. 'It is very late. Goodnight, my lord.'

She hurried towards the door, but Lord Rutherford stood up and put out his arm to halt her flight. 'I think you have lost your sense of direction,' he said with a curious half-smile twisting his mouth. 'Perhaps you are not aware that you are running full tilt towards my bedroom.'

'I did not mean . . . You must not think . . .' She tried to push past him in the opposite direction, but he refused to let her go and once again she found herself held prisoner in his arms.

'What must I not think?' he murmured. 'That you are an intolerable temptation? That your mother trained you far too well in the subtle skills of her profession? Is that what I must not think?'

'I've already told you I can't sing,' she murmured helplessly. 'What has my mother's profession to do with anything?'

'At this moment, nothing at all,' he said. As he spoke, his arms tightened their hold and she felt the firm spread of his fingers press against her spine and the buttons of his waistcoat crushed into the softness of her breasts. If she had been able to think clearly, she would have pulled herself out of his embrace, but before she could do anything, he put a hand beneath her chin, tilting her face up and looking at her searchingly. She found herself unable to turn away from his gaze. His eyes appeared darker than she had ever seen them and they were heavy with some emotion that she didn't understand. He stroked his hand down her cheek in a swift, light caress, and a flush rippled under her skin, making her face burn beneath his touch.

'You're trembling,' he said.

She realised that he spoke the truth. She had never in her life before felt faint, but now she was forced to lean heavily against him to prevent herself from falling. She lay within the circle of his arms, and fought against the urge to nuzzle her cheek against the starched white front of his evening shirt.

'You are a very desirable woman,' he said huskily, and his mouth was so close to hers that she felt the whisper of his breath against her lips. He cupped her face in his hands again, brushing his thumb softly across her mouth. Slowly, he bent his head and touched his lips to hers and she felt the shock of his kiss right through her body. She couldn't think what to do, so she simply stood there, her heart thudding but her lips tightly closed. His kiss slowly deepened and she became frightened by the strange urgency of the sensations he was arousing inside her. With a sudden surge of energy, she tore herself away from his arms.

'Please, my lord . . .' she said. 'My lord, you must not . . .'

There was a moment of tense silence. 'No,' he said at last. 'You are quite right. Indeed I must not.' He swung round and walked back to the fire, keeping his face averted. 'Goodnight, Deborah.'

Irrationally, she didn't want him to part from her with such abruptness. She was aware of a peculiar jerkiness in her breathing and a feverish racing of her pulses. Now that he was so far away from her, she felt an inexplicable longing to return to his arms. 'My lord? . . .' she whispered.

He did not turn round. 'Go to your room,' he said. 'Go now.'

She was bewildered by the curtness of his command and the harshness of his voice. She hurried across the sitting-room to her bedroom, casting only a brief glance in his direction. He, too, seemed anxious to avoid her gaze. He stood at the hearth, staring into the fire, his hand poised with apparent casualness upon the mantelpiece.

The casualness vanished the moment Deborah's bedroom door finally closed. His shoulders slumped forward, revealing the extent of self-control he had needed to exercise in order to conceal his true emotions. The cool indifference disappeared from his face and he pressed his hand to his eyes in a gesture indicative of extreme weariness. The glow of the dying fire revealed the tautness around his mouth and the haunting bleakness of his eyes.

He straightened up and stared silently at the closed door of his wife's room. He took two steps forward, then, with a small exclamation of disgust, swung on his heel and walked quickly, determinedly, into his own bedroom.

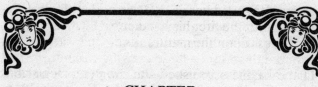

CHAPTER
NINE

DEBORAH DECLINED to eat breakfast the next morning and thus managed to avoid all private conversation with her husband until they were in the carriage, driving to his mother's house. The events of the previous night remained vividly in her mind, causing her to blush bright scarlet every time she remembered the way she had behaved. In the cool light of day, she couldn't imagine what had happened to her. She sat in the far corner of the carriage and made sure that nothing she wore, not even the hem of her gown, was in contact with any portion of her husband's anatomy.

Lord Rutherford, she soon discovered, was no more anxious to initiate a conversation than she was. He stared out of the carriage window with grim determination, observing the busy streets with as much intensity as if he had never before set foot in London. He did not appear to notice that she was wearing her elegant grey tippet and her new bonnet trimmed with pink rosebuds.

Neither of them spoke until the carriage drew to a halt outside an imposing mansion in Cavendish Square. 'This is my mother's house,' said Lord Rutherford, breaking their long silence as he assisted her from the carriage. 'She inherited it from Lord Grayden, her father.'

He said nothing more until the butler had ushered them into a large drawing-room furnished in the height of fashion with overstuffed, button-back chairs, a red velour sofa trimmed with gold tassels, six or seven velvet-draped tables and two towering glass domes of polished wax fruit, one of which must have been close to eight feet tall. Deborah's first startled thought was that even Cousin George's house, recently decorated throughout in Balmoral tartan and red Turkish carpets, contained no room quite as hideous.

The Dowager Lady Rutherford stood in front of the fire, resplendent in a pale blue morning-gown of softest wool. She was a faded blonde beauty already past fifty, still elegant, although much decorated with strings of pearls and large gold brooches. Her hands fluttered in welcome, artfully displaying the layers of white lace that decorated the inside of her frilled sleeves. 'Welcome, you naughty children,' she said as soon as they stepped into the room. 'You both deserve to be scolded, but I shall have to forgive you because I am so excited that you are here. How could you marry without telling me of your plans? Bring your bride closer, John, so that I may see what a delightful daughter you have chosen for me.'

Lord Rutherford escorted Deborah to his mother's side, skilfully negotiating a passageway between two dark green wing-chairs and a pair of bloated aspidistras. He halted in front of his mother, leaning forward to bestow a dutiful kiss.

Deborah noticed that he took care not to crush the front of his mother's gown and that the Dowager moved slightly so that her son's kiss did not actually make contact with the discreet maquillage covering her cheeks.

There was a note of restraint in Lord Rutherford's voice as he made the introduction. 'This is Deborah, Mama. I know how pleased you will be to welcome her to our family.'

The Dowager took Deborah's hands into a light clasp. 'Of course I am pleased,' she said, kissing the air about three inches away from Deborah's ear. 'I have been telling John for years that he needed to marry, and I am delighted that he has chosen a girl who is so beautiful. He tells me you haven't yet bought your trousseau and I can't wait to come shopping with you. The bonnet you are wearing is simply charming—I know we shall have a wonderful time together. I love shopping, don't you? The London stores are so exciting, not at all like the dreary little shops in Salisbury. That is the nearest town to Rutherford Place, you know, but I never go there if I can help it. There is nothing in Salisbury but a cathedral and one is obliged to call on the bishop and take tea with the archdeacon. I loathe the country, don't you? It is so full of sheep and cows and people who want to talk about them. How can one talk about sheep, I ask you? After all, there is absolutely nothing interesting one can say about a sheep.'

'Possibly not,' Deborah agreed, when the Dowager finally paused to draw breath. 'Although the size of the wool crop must be important to farmers.'

'Farmers!' The Dowager shuddered delicately. 'When I was a girl, people one knew were simply never farmers. Now *everybody* seems to feel obliged to discuss seed drills and rotary tillers.' She walked over to the bell-rope and tugged it firmly. 'We shall have some sherry,' she said when the butler appeared. She did not wait for the door to close before saying, 'Now, Deborah, you shall tell me exactly how you and John came to fall in love. I am longing to hear *everything*! I confess, I had almost given up hope of seeing my son married. I swear he has ignored every débutante I have ever presented to him. Tell me, how long have you known each other?'

'For quite some time,' Deborah said, blushing at the lie. 'It was not possible to marry right away for . . . for family reasons.'

As she spoke, Lord Rutherford smiled at her with apparent fondness. 'Having seen Deborah, Mama, you will understand why all those débutantes of yours failed to captivate me. My heart was already lost.'

With a supreme effort, Deborah managed to prevent her mouth falling open. The Dowager, fortunately, seemed unaware of her daughter-in-law's astonishment. She gave a happy trill of laughter just as the butler returned with the tray of sherry. 'You see, my dear, how completely you have captivated my son! And this is the man who was declared unconquerable! Thank you, Horten, you may pour us each some sherry and then we shan't need you any more.'

She continued to chatter cheerfully until

Deborah lifted her glass to take a sip of sherry. 'But where is your betrothal ring?' the Dowager demanded. 'Didn't John give you my mother's emeralds?'

Deborah nearly dropped her wine-glass. 'Your mother's emeralds?' she mumbled, waiting hopefully for Lord Rutherford to rescue her from an impossible situation. No help was forthcoming. 'Er . . . no, Lady Rutherford,' she said, before the silence could become too conspicuous. 'Your son chose a new betrothal ring for me . . . but it was . . . it was a little too large and it has been returned to the jeweller so that it can be made tighter.'

'Yes, I see that your fingers are very slender. What is the ring like?'

Deborah's powers of invention gave out completely. She stared at her husband in desperate, silent appeal. 'I chose sapphires, Mama,' he said coolly. 'It was the best I could do, although the stones still do not quite compare with the brilliance of Deborah's eyes.'

'Sapphires,' the Dowager said. 'Of course. Your taste, John, is always impeccable. The emeralds would have been hopeless.' She leaned gracefully against the back of her chair. 'Oh, isn't this cosy! Deborah, you must tell me *exactly* where you met my son. All my friends are utterly amazed to think that London's most determined bachelor has succumbed at last. They are dying to meet you and they will be so charmed when they see the pair of you together—such a handsome couple! Where did you say you met, my dear?'

Deborah once again found herself at a loss for

words. She looked at her husband with a hint of defiance in her gaze. 'Perhaps, my dear John, you would like to explain to your mother how we met.'

'Certainly, my dear Deborah.' Lord Rutherford's gaze was subtly mocking, and a faint flush of colour washed into her cheeks. He stared at her for a second or so, a strange expression in his eyes, before he turned to his mother with a polite, impersonal smile. 'I met Deborah some time ago when she was working as a lady volunteer with a relief committee in Lancashire. Many of the poorer people in that part of the country are suffering great hardship at the moment because of the cotton shortage caused by the war in America.'

'Oh,' said the Dowager, clearly disappointed by such a prosaic first encounter. 'That is certainly a very unusual way to meet. And what, may I ask, has that tiresome war in America to do with the labourers in Lancashire?'

'Most of the raw cotton we use in our English factories is grown in the Confederacy,' Deborah said, relieved to have a question she could answer without telling any more lies. 'Unfortunately, the war between the various American states is proving very bitter, and the Confederate plantation-owners have no time to tend to their cotton-fields. In any case, their merchant ships cannot break out of the Union blockade. Consequently, almost no raw cotton is reaching English shores and many of our mills have been forced to close. As you can imagine, the suffering among the weavers who are thrown out of work is great.'

A slight frown wrinkled the powdered smooth-

ness of the Dowager's brow. 'I don't understand,'
she said, with a charming little laugh. 'But let us not
talk about such horrid subjects. Commerce is
always incomprehensible to a lady, I think.' She
flashed Deborah another sweet smile. 'You must
be careful, my dear, that you don't give people
cause to think that you have opinions about matters
which ladies should never understand.'

Deborah clenched her hands tightly. 'I believe,
Lady Rutherford, that when children are starving it
is the duty of every educated person to understand
why.'

'But my dear Deborah, one needs only to take
the children some soup, there is no need to enquire
why they are hungry! And an English lady can
never need to understand what is happening in
America! If, by some extraordinary chance, events
in that country do happen to have an effect upon
our lives, it will be your husband's duty to understand what is going on. You have merely to listen to
his explanations and then to accept his opinions.
And John has explanations for *everything*. You are
so pretty, my dear, that it is especially dangerous
for you to think. You will give yourself a fever of
the brain if you try to understand issues that the
Lord clearly did not intend any lady to compre-
hend, particularly a pretty one.'

'I am not aware, Lady Rutherford, that the Lord
at any time stipulated that a woman is forbidden to
use the intelligence He himself gave her.'

The Dowager's hands fluttered with even more
agitation than before. 'But of course it is forbidden!
It is in the Bible, I am sure of it. And if it isn't, well

then it certainly ought to be. I shall speak to the archbishop about it the next time I see him. It is a woman's duty never to think if there is a man available to think for her. That is why we ladies marry, so that we shall always have somebody to protect us. Is that no so, John?'

'Undoubtedly,' he said, his voice very dry. 'I am sure there could be no better reason. Mama, may I remind you of your kind suggestion that we should accompany you to the Royal Opera House at the end of this week? Deborah wishes to purchase a new gown for the occasion, and she would be most grateful if you would give her your advice.'

The frown disappeared from the Dowager's brow and was immediately replaced by a delighted smile. 'The Opera! How could I have forgotten! We shall go out right away, Deborah, and order the most perfect gown for you from Louise. Perhaps oyster satin . . . I have a wonderful new dress in gold silk. Oh, what marvellous fun we shall have! How happy I am that you are married, John!'

'And I am delighted that you are pleased. However, on that ecstatic note, Mama, I believe that I must bid you goodbye. I am due at the House within the hour, but I shall take a cab and leave the carriage for you two ladies.' He bowed formally over his mother's white fingers, then turned to Deborah and tucked her hand into his arm, drawing her determinedly into the hallway. He spoke to her softly as they walked to the front door. 'Your allowance will not be sufficient to cover the cost of clothes suitable for the Opera,' he said. 'But please buy whatever my mother recommends, and don't worry about the price. The dressmaker will automatically send the bill direct to me.' There was a brief pause, and he looked away when he began to speak again. 'My mother's taste in clothes is exquisite.' His voice was devoid of all expression. 'You should not hesitate to follow her advice.'

Deborah understood that he would come no closer to admitting that his mother's judgment in other matters was severely lacking. 'I shall be happy to listen to the Dowager's recommendations,' she said.

Lord Rutherford retrieved his hat and overcoat from the footman. 'Thank you,' he said and went quickly down the marble steps.

Margaret fluffed up the fragile ruffle of écru lace that trimmed the low neckline of Deborah's evening-gown, then gave one last shake to the double-frilled hem. The ivory taffeta rustled softly as it fell in place over the stiffened layers of silk petticoats, and the maid gave a satisfied sigh.

'It is perfect, my lady,' she said shyly. 'Everything is perfect. You'll outshine all the ladies at the Opera tonight.'

'I wish I could believe you, Margaret, but I'm afraid you are an expert flatterer!'

'Not so, my lady, I promise you.'

Deborah glanced into the mirror, hoping the maid had not exaggerated too much. She touched the narrow band of cream silk rosebuds which confined her curls behind her ears, wondering if the simple style was formal enough for a gala performance at the Opera. Until recently, she had never cared whether or not people considered her beautiful, but tonight she wanted desperately to look her best. Not only because it was her début in London society, but because she wanted Lord Rutherford to say . . . she wanted him to feel . . . She cut the jumbled thoughts off sharply and swung away from the mirror just as a knock sounded at the door.

Margaret opened the door and curtsied as her master walked in, magnificent in formal black evening clothes. Deborah discovered that her throat was dry as she watched her husband aproach.

He came to a halt while still several feet away from her. 'You may leave us, Margaret,' he said. He waited until the door clicked shut behind the maid before he spoke. 'You look superb, Deborah,' he said quietly. 'I do not believe I have ever seen a more beautiful woman.'

His words caused a tingle of excitement to ripple under her skin. 'Thank you,' she murmured. 'The Dowager was sure you would like this dress.'

'It is you, not the . . . That is to say, the dress is splendid. I understand my mother's dressmaker is considered one of the best in London.' He turned slightly away from her and reached into his pocket to extract a small jeweller's box.

'I have something to give you,' he said abruptly. 'It was careless of me not to think of it earlier, before my mother noticed the omission.' He flipped open the black velvet box and revealed a betrothal ring of star sapphires, set in a circle of diamonds.

Her first instinct was to refuse it, because there

was nothing of tenderness or affection in her husband's manner which would give meaning to such an expensive gift. But he gave her no chance to express her doubts. He took her left hand into his, and slipped the dazzling circlet of jewels on her finger. When the ring was in place, he glanced at it briefly. 'It looks very well,' he said, his voice indifferent.

Deborah stared at her hand in silence. 'You are . . . generous, my lord,' she said at last. 'And I am grateful for your thoughtfulness.'

He frowned, as though for some reason her reaction did not satisfy him. 'I have another small gift for you.' He reached into the inner pocket of his evening coat and withdrew a second velvet box, considerably larger than the first. He flicked it open and casually displayed a necklace of entwined sapphires and diamonds, designed to look like a chain of flowers. He dropped the shimmering coil of jewels into Deborah's hands. 'The jeweller assures me it will look well with the betrothal ring.'

'My lord . . . I cannot . . . You should not . . .'

'Please put it on,' he said.

She held the glittering gems against her neck and turned to the mirror, glad of an excuse to tear her eyes away from Lord Rutherford's disturbing gaze. She tried to fasten the tiny, pearl-encrusted clasp, but her fingers were shaking so much that she couldn't manage to slide the intricate gold hooks together.

Suddenly Lord Rutherford was standing close behind her. 'Allow me to assist you,' he said, his voice and expression equally stripped of any emotion.

Silently, she handed him the necklace and bent her head forward. He lifted the thick cluster of curls from her neck, and his hands felt warm against the icy coldness of her skin. As soon as he had fastened the clasp, he tilted her head upright. 'Look in the mirror,' he commanded softly.

The jewels encircled her throat in a delicate blaze of blue fire, emphasising the unusual colour of her eyes and the faint pink flush in her cheeks. She looked at the necklace, then at Lord Rutherford's hands, which still rested against her shoulders. His fingers appeared darkly tanned against the whiteness of her skin. 'The necklace is beautiful, my lord,' she whispered.

He said nothing. For a long, silent moment they looked at one another in the mirror, then he twisted her in his arms and with agonising slowness bent his head towards her.

At the touch of his mouth against her lips she felt a leap of feverish excitement, a sensation so fierce that she wasn't even sure it was pleasant. She parted her lips in a tiny gasp of astonishment and immediately—incredibly—felt the flick of his tongue inside her mouth. She was so shocked by the extraordinary intimacy of the sensation that for a few seconds her entire body seemed paralysed. Then, as the shock faded, she felt an inexplicable longing to respond to the passion of his embrace. She wished she knew how to make him experience the same restless yearning that she herself was feeling. She curled her hands against the stiffness of his evening shirt and felt the beat of his heart through the thin linen, thudding rapidly beneath

her palms. Hesitantly, she closed her eyes, sur-
rendering herself to the increasing passion of his
kiss.

For a moment, his arms tightened demandingly
around her—then, abruptly, he dragged himself
away, walking from her with rapid strides. When he
turned back to her, his expression was already
entirely controlled, although his face was white and
his eyes were dark with concealed emotions.

'I must beg your pardon,' he said formally. 'I can
give you no adequate excuse for my behaviour.'

Deborah stared determinedly at the floor. 'We
are married,' she said. 'I understand that it is
perfectly proper . . . that is to say, I had heard . . .
I have been told that married persons are at liberty
to . . . to embrace one another if they so wish.'

'But we agreed that our marriage would not be
consummated,' he said curtly. 'Therefore, please
accept my assurances that such incidents as you
have just endured will not—cannot—occur in the
future.'

Deborah did not raise her eyes from the floor.
'My cloak is in the dressing-room,' she said. 'I shall
join you in a moment.' She walked out of the
bedroom, wondering what her husband would say
if he knew that she longed for his kisses and that
she derived no pleasure at all from his repeated
promises that their marriage would never be
consummated.

It was three years since Deborah had been to the
Opera; three years since she had heard her mother
sing in Mozart's *Don Giovanni*, just before a

typhoid epidemic in Naples killed both her parents. She discovered as she drove into Covent Garden that the anguish of their death had faded at last and she entered the Royal Italian Opera House with a wonderful feeling of coming home. Tonight, she thought, nothing would be capable of dimming her pleasure in Verdi's glorious music, not even the painful tension of her relationship with her husband. Her parents had considered *Il Trovatore* to be Verdi's masterpiece and the role of Leonora had been one of her mother's favourites. Deborah looked forward to hearing it for the first time.

She gazed admiringly at the blazing lights of the foyer, the opulent crimson hangings, the elegant clothes of the audience, then gave a sigh of supreme happiness. She wished her parents could be here with her, but the wish no longer carried with it the bitter sting of grief. 'Isn't it heavenly?' she said to Lord Rutherford, forgetting the scene in her bedroom in the excitement of the moment.

'Indeed,' he said. 'Overheated rooms, inferior champagne and uncomfortable clothes. The feminine version of Paradise.'

She laughed up at him, and for one brief moment saw an answering gleam of amusement flash into his eyes. For a split second it was as though they were alone in the crowded foyer, then the Dowager spoke and the intimate moment was gone.

Deborah sat entranced through the first act and, when the interval arrived, her sparkling happiness helped to protect her from nervousness as the Dowager introduced her to a succession of formidable society matrons. Deborah acknowledged the

introductions gracefully and talked quietly about
the performance, comparing the soprano with
Queen Victoria's favourite, Miss Jenny Lind. She
parried questions about her background with a
sweet smile and a skilful changing of the subject.
Whenever possible, she deferred politely to the
Dowager, and was spared any need to cope with
Lord Rutherford's presence because the crush of
people waiting to be introduced made it impossible
for her husband to get near her.

By the second interval, Society had officially
decreed that the new Lady Rutherford was a
charming girl. The Dowager whispered to several
privileged older matrons that the attachment between her son and Miss Phipps had been of long
standing, and the matrons—delighted to be the
recipients of a confidence—universally declared
that it was no wonder Lord Rutherford had not
wanted to make do with a second-best débutante.
The Dowager fluttered her fan, and accepted con-
gratulations on her enchanting daughter-in-law
exactly as though she had personally arranged the
match. Indeed, by the end of the evening, she was
beginning to think that she had.

When the opera was finally over, the Dowager
embraced Deborah effusively, for once paying no
heed to the crushing of her gold silk gown. 'My
dear, you were such a success!' she said. 'If only the
Queen would come out of mourning for that
wretched Albert, whom absolutely nobody liked
anyway. Then I could present you at Court and you
would be set for *anything*. The Prince of Wales is
just not the same as the Queen, you know.'

Deborah politely agreed with the indisputable truth of this statement, and a footman announced the arrival of their carriages beneath the main portico. The Dowager climbed into her brougham, still showering compliments on Deborah. Life, it seemed, could hold no greater joy than a beautiful daughter-in-law who was also socially gracious.

Deborah was every bit as happy as the Dowager, although for somewhat different reasons. Social success was not particularly important to her, but she was glad she had not disgraced her husband or offended his mother. She was pleased that London Society had found her beautiful, and that her gown had been admired. Above all, she was intoxicated by the music and high drama of the opera. It was as if the dreary, puritan years with Cousin George had rolled away, and she was once again the much-loved only daughter of affectionate, frolicsome parents.

'Wasn't it marvellous?' she said to Lord Rutherford as their carriage rolled through the gas-lit streets towards home. 'I have had such a wonderful time!' She hummed a snatch of one of the arias, hopelessly off-key, not noticing the lines of strain tightening her husband's mouth. 'Did you see the tenor during the last act, when he must pretend to be dying? I thought *I* would die laughing when he kept popping up from the floor to sing another flourishing trill! I am sure all those embellishments are not in the original score.'

'I suppose the tenor was a better singer than he was actor,' Lord Rutherford agreed.

'They usually are! I don't know what it is about

tenors that causes them to feel every gesture must be larger than life. And their temperaments make most sopranos seem easy-going. You cannot imagine the scenes I have watched some tenors enact on days when they feel they are not quite in voice.' She laughed and hummed another aria even less tunefully than the previous one. 'Oh, I think I could watch opera all night, and never get tired of it. Isn't that strange, my lord, when my mother always said that I had a voice like a crow?'

'Yes,' he said.

The carriage came to a halt outside the Rutherford house and Deborah sprang out, scarcely waiting for the assistance of the footman. She ran up the stairs, her velvet cloak billowing out behind her. She did not halt until she arrived, laughing and breathless, in their private sitting-room.

Lord Rutherford followed her into the room, leaving the door into the hallway open. 'Goodnight, Deborah,' he said as he began to walk towards his dressing-room. 'I am pleased that you enjoyed the evening. I believe it must be accounted a success, from all points of view.'

'Oh, but you cannot go to bed so early!' Deborah exclaimed. 'It is scarcely midnight and the night is still young. An opera should be merely the beginning of a merry evening. Now it is time for us to be dancing, and drinking champagne.'

'I have no wish to dance with you,' he said curtly. 'And it seems to me that you have already consumed quite enough champagne. Goodnight.'

'Oh, you cannot wish to be such a spoilsport!' she exclaimed, seizing his hands. 'Let us dance in here, since we can't go to a party. I shall hum the music and you shall be my partner.'

She went laughingly into his arms and his entire body immediately became utterly still. The tension surrounding him reached out and enveloped her, seeming to grow until it filled the whole room. She pulled herself away from him as if she had been burned by the contact with his body, and they stared at one another across a foot of space that suddenly seemed as wide and unbridgeable as an abyss.

It was Lord Rutherford who broke the unbearable silence. 'I think, as I said before, that we should not dance. I bid you goodnight, Deborah.'

'Goodnight, my lord,' she murmured and something in her voice caused him to halt on the threshold of the room although he did not come back to her. 'What is the matter, Deborah?' he asked. 'What do you want of me?'

The truthful answer was that she had no idea what it was that she wanted. She knew only that she craved his presence and yearned for his touch. She wondered if her own face revealed the same tormented longing she could see written so plainly in the depths of his eyes. 'It is my necklace,' she said finally, and she knew that her voice sounded strangely husky when she spoke. 'I need your help to unfasten the clasp.'

'You should summon a maid to assist you.'

'I gave them all permission to go to bed.'

'You should not have done so,' he said. 'You will need help to take off your dress.' She did not reply and he walked slowly across the room. 'Turn round,' he ordered harshly, 'and please hold your hair out of my way.'

She obeyed his command. She could feel that his hands were not perfectly steady as he unfastened the clasp of her necklace, and her pulses began to race with a bewildering, tantalising excitement.

'It is done,' he said, placing the necklace on a near-by table.

'Thank you.' She turned to face him, no longer attempting to conceal the turbulent state of her emotions.

'Deborah,' he said tersely. 'Do not look at me so.' Even as he spoke, he trailed his fingers lightly across her shoulders and she quivered in response to his caress. When he bent his head to kiss her, she parted her lips willingly. It seemed as though her body had been waiting a lifetime for the pleasure of his touch.

He ended the embrace with such abruptness that she felt as though her mouth had been torn away from his. She gave a soft murmur of protest, wanting him to take her back into the warm comfort of his arms. She swayed involuntarily towards his strength and leaned her head against his satin waistcoat, knowing instinctively that only he could assuage the strange yearning that threatened to overwhelm her. 'Please . . .' she whispered. 'Please, my lord, kiss me again.'

'No!' He turned his head away, then quickly turned back and kissed her with a fierce, consuming urgency. 'Perhaps this once it would not matter if I made love to you,' he murmured between kisses. 'Perhaps, having taken you to my bed, I could put you from my mind. Oh God, Deborah, why did I choose to torment myself by making you my wife?'

'But I am not yet your wife,' she said. 'Except in name.'

Her words fell between them into a little pool of silence then, with a harsh exclamation, he swept her into his arms and strode across the room. He pushed open the door and carried her across to his bed. 'Tonight I shall make you my wife,' he said, as he laid her down on the embroidered covers. 'Just for once, I shall forget all about honour and duty.' He cradled her in his arms, trailing kisses over her bare shoulders. 'Oh, yes!' he groaned. 'Tonight I shall think only of how much I want you.' He reached out and smoothed a stray curl away from her face and for a moment it seemed to Deborah that tenderness replaced the desire darkening his eyes. 'I promise you we shall make this a night to remember,' he said softly.

He gathered her into his arms, whispering soft words of love. He caressed her gently, expertly, until the world faded from her consciousness and there was only the darkness binding them together and, finally, the star-bright ecstasy of his possession.

CHAPTER
TEN

A SLIGHT SOUND caused Deborah to stir and she was immediately awake, although the grey light filtering through the curtains suggested that it was scarcely dawn. When she realised that she was alone in the bed she sat up quickly, looking round the room for Lord Rutherford.

She saw him at once. He was already dressed in formal morning clothes, standing by the window, apparently lost in contemplation of the sunrise. Some instinct must have warned him that Deborah was awake, for he turned round and looked silently towards the bed.

Her heart immediately sank. Even in the dim light of early morning, she could see how withdrawn he appeared. It seemed as though nothing remained of the passionate, tender man who had repeatedly made love to her the night before. This morning his expression was unreadable, his emotions closed behind the mask of cool arrogance he knew so well how to assume. The rigidity of his posture simply underlined the general impression of remoteness.

They looked at one another for several moments without speaking, and Deborah became aware of the deep lines of strain etched behind her husband's blank expression. She began to consider the possibility that, for all the apparent hauteur of his appearance, her husband might be vulnerable to hurt at her hands.

His first words dispelled the illusion. 'I have brought a robe from your room,' he said, not bothering with any form of greeting. 'Perhaps you would be good enough to put it on.'

She felt a wave of humiliation wash over her body as she realised that she was still naked beneath the covers. Lord Rutherford came over to the bed and held out her robe. She quickly slipped into it, tying the satin belt tightly around her waist, and closing the buttons all the way up to the neck before she got out of bed. She avoided looking at him as she walked towards her own room. She had nothing she wanted to say to this cold, disapproving stranger.

'Please don't leave,' he said. 'There are . . . certain things . . . we must discuss.'

'My maid will be arriving . . . I don't want her to see . . .'

'I have already put all the clothes you were wearing last night into your dressing-room and I have made sure that your bed appears to have been slept in.'

'You have been very busy while I slept, have you not?'

There was a moment of silence. 'Yes,' he said finally. 'I found sleep—elusive—last night.' He fell silent again, pacing the room restlessly until he came to a halt at her side. 'Deborah, I am obliged to offer you an apology. I did not know . . . The circumstances in which I first found you . . . It had not occurred to me that you might never have . . .' He drew a deep breath. 'In short, what I am trying to say is that I had not suspected you to be a virgin. Had I known the truth I would never have allowed the situation last night to get so badly out of hand.'

'It is the—duty—of a married woman to submit to her husband,' she said without looking at him.

'But I had absolved you from that duty by the promises I made when we married. Last night's events cannot—must not—occur again. You have my assurance, Deborah, that there will never be a repetition of what happened last night.'

'You have made such promises before.'

'But this time they will not be broken.'

She stared at her hands, which were twisted into a single tight ball of tension. 'What if . . . what if I said that I wished to be a true wife to you, my lord?' He made no reply, so she swallowed her pride and stumbled on. 'I was an only child and then I was orphaned before my sixteenth birthday, so you see I have always longed to be part of a family.' She stared even more fixedly at her hands. 'M-my wifely d-duties are not necessarily burdensome to me, my lord.'

He turned away so abruptly that she thought he was going to leave the room. He kept his face averted when he replied to her. 'Your feelings are a matter of indifference to me,' he said. 'I have told you many times that I have no wish for a proper wife. I made my situation perfectly plain to you at the time we agreed to this marriage.'

'But what am I supposed to do for the rest of my life?' she asked. 'How am I supposed to fill my days if I am to be no more than a glorified household decoration?'

He smiled with deliberate, hurtful cynicism. 'I have no doubt that you will soon learn to substitute the pleasures of spending my money for the more doubtful pleasures of raising a family.'

'Do you think so?' she cried angrily. 'I fear you don't know me very well, my lord. It is true you told me many times that you had no wish for a proper wife and I was foolish enough to accept the terms of your offer. The fear of starvation can persuade us to do many things we would not otherwise contemplate. But I am no longer quite so hungry or quite so frightened and I think it is my turn to ask *you* a question. Why did you marry me?'

He turned round at last, his expression lacking any trace of warmth or kindness. 'There seems no particular reason why you should not be told the truth,' he said with a shrug. 'Under the terms of my great-grandfather's will, a Rutherford heir cannot touch the capital of the estate until he is married. My father left capital funds in excess of a million pounds but, as a bachelor, I could not use them. They remained locked in a banker's trust. Since my father's death, the family lands in Somerset have been suffering under an increasing burden of debt. I needed my father's money, my dear, and that is why I needed a wife. There was no other reason. My mother, who was aware of my financial straits, thrust one débutante after another in my direction, but I did not wish to find myself saddled with any of

them. The married state is not one which greatly
appeals to me. That is why I decided to marry you,
a woman without connections or social position, a
woman whom I could safely ignore. Unfortunately,
I did not realise that I was encumbering myself with
a bride who would constantly nag for my attention.
I could have married a débutante if I wished to be
nagged.'

'And what of love and affection?' she whispered.
'Have you no need for that?'

'I am well supplied with mistresses,' he said
cruelly. 'I have no need for the naive embraces of a
virgin bride. I prefer to make love to a woman who
is experienced enough to give me pleasure, and
sensible enough not to pester me with her problems. Fortunately, there is no clause in my great-
grandfather's will which says that I must endure the
attentions of my bride once I am married.'

'I see,' she said. 'I . . . regret . . . that I have been
such a demanding wife, my lord.'

She was so hurt by his words that she felt temporarily paralysed. She could not seem to move from
the place where she was standing. Lord Rutherford
stared at her for a second or two, then swung
violently away and strode towards his dressing-
room. Her heart began to pound as she watched
him go and her throat felt tight with unshed tears.
Scarcely knowing why she spoke or why she called
to him, she murmured his name.

At the sound of her voice he turned and, after a
moment's hesitation, came back to stand in front of
her. He hesitated again and then, as if acting
against his better judgment, he gently tipped up her

chin and touched his hand to her cheek in a swift,
delicate caress. It seemed to Deborah that, despite
all his harsh words, his eyes glowed with deep,
caring tenderness. She stretched out her hand to
touch him but he immediately turned away.

'Your maid will soon be bringing in your tea-
tray,' he said coolly. 'I will bid you good morning,
madam.'

The door of his dressing-room slammed shut,
and there was nothing left for Deborah to do but
gather the tattered shreds of her dignity and walk
quietly into her own bedroom.

During the ensuing weeks, Deborah often mar-
velled at the fact that two people could live in the
same house and see so little of each other. Lord
Rutherford spent his days in the House of Lords
and usually returned late at night, long after she
had gone to bed. She filled her days with domestic
chores, gradually asserting her control over the
army of servants and transforming the gloomy
town-house into a comfortable home in which to
live. She and her husband breakfasted separately in
their own bedrooms and ate together only when the
Dowager was invited to join them for dinner, or
when the Dowager gave a dinner-party and asked
them to attend. On such occasions, Lord Rutherford was a model of courtesy while they were on
public display. Once they were alone, he retreated
behind a wall of silence that was impossible to
penetrate.

The demands of running so large a household
should have kept Deborah fully occupied. Instead,

she found time crawling past on leaden feet and the ache in her heart grew a little more painful with each passing day. It was early December when she finally found an explanation for her state of malaise. She was glancing through *The Times* when she came upon an editorial praising a speech Lord Rutherford had made on the problems of young women working in the Lancashire cotton mills. She was deeply impressed by the wisdom of his comments and the compassion of his recommendations. She found herself longing to speak to him in person, to tell him how much she admired his efforts on behalf of the unemployed. She thought longingly of the early days of their marriage when they had spent hours talking together over the dinner-table, their food growing cold on their plates as they explored each other's ideas. Looking back, she thought wistfully that she had never known another man who could make her feel so alive simply by being in the same room with her.

Hard on the heels of this thought came a realisation that had been hovering on the edges of her consciousness for weeks. She was in love with Lord Rutherford. It was his presence that brought colour to her world. It was his absence that caused her days to lose their meaning. She smiled bitterly at the extent of her own folly. How could she have been foolish enough to fall in love with her own husband, a man who quite obviously despised her and longed to be free of her presence? Moreover, despite the fact that she knew no virtuous woman ever derived pleasure from the obligations of the marriage-bed, she finally admitted to herself that she longed for her husband's lovemaking with a fierce, aching need that gave her no rest. Her mind craved his company and her body craved his touch. The uncomfortable self-knowledge, once it had thrust itself into her awareness, would not go away.

She could not fall asleep that night, although she counted thousands of sheep jumping over stiles and clambering through gaps in hedgerows. She did not realise what was causing her insomnia until she heard the sound of her husband's footsteps in the corridor outside her room. Then she immediately knew what she had been waiting for. She got out of bed, slipping her robe round her shoulders, waiting in the darkness until she heard the valet bid a final goodnight to his master.

When the house was completely silent again, she thrust her feet into swansdown-trimmed slippers and crossed the sitting-room to her husband's room. She knocked softly on his door. There was no response, so she opened the door and walked slowly into the room.

He was seated in a wing-chair pulled close to the fire, wearing a dark blue brocade dressing-gown. A large decanter of brandy rested on a table close to his side. He stood up as she approached, and for a moment she thought she detected a flare of deep emotion in his eyes. She decided it must only have been a trick of the firelight, for when she came nearer she realised that his expression was as cold and indifferent as ever.

'I am . . . I am sorry to disturb you,' she said. 'Please sit down.'

He inclined his head as he returned to his chair. He stared into the fire. 'What may I do for you?'

'Nothing, I just wanted to talk. I have read so many complimentary accounts of your work in Parliament and I wanted you to know . . . I wanted to express my admiration for the efforts you are making on behalf of all those women and children who have no power to speak for themselves.'

'Thank you. It is gratifying to see how smoothly the latest Factory Art is moving through Committee.'

She sat on a small footstool close to his chair, all too aware of her husband's attractions and the intimacy of their situation. It suddenly occurred to her that there was no longer the smallest reason to keep the details of her past secret from him. She wanted to be honest with him so that there would be hope of changing the basis of their marriage. She found herself speaking almost before the decision to confide in him was consciously made.

'I have never told you why I first became interested in factory legislation,' she said.

He swirled his cognac slowly in his glass. 'You have no obligation to confide in me, Deborah.'

'But I would like to tell you something about my family. It is because of my cousin that I know how desperately reforms are still needed. I have already mentioned that my mother was an opera-singer, but I didn't tell you that my father was the only son of a small Yorkshire landowner, and the grandson of a baronet. My mother was disowned by her parents after her marriage, so when my parents died, I was sent home from Italy to live with my father's cousin. He is the inheritor of the family baronetcy, and an extremely prosperous mill-owner. The rest of the family are elderly and they all agreed that I was very fortunate to be taken in by Cousin George. I can't blame them for not wanting to offer a home to a sixteen-year-old girl who spoke Italian more readily than English, and who once outraged an entire dinner-table by announcing that she liked baked octopus better than grilled trout. As you can imagine, everybody was delighted when Cousin George announced that he would marry me on my nineteenth birthday. I was not given much say in the matter because my opinions, naturally, seemed somewhat irrelevant to the matters under consideration.'

Lord Rutherford's hand shook slightly as he replaced his cognac on the table. 'Are you telling me, by any chance, that the waif I picked up on my doorstep—that you are the cousin of a prosperous baronet?'

'Perhaps you don't believe me,' she said. 'I know it seems incredible.'

He laughed harshly. 'Oh no,' he said. 'I believe you. In view of some of the other things that I have discovered recently, these revelations seem no more than a quite minor disaster. But don't allow me to interrupt your story. Please continue, I am fascinated.'

'Cousin George took me on a tour of his mills, my lord. I had always known he was a man who cared greatly about material possessions, but I had never before realised precisely how he acquired his wealth. The sights in those factories we toured will haunt me for the rest of my life. I don't need to describe them to you, I am sure. Simply imagine the worst mills you have seen, and there you have the perfect picture of how Cousin George made his money. I could not marry such a man, of course, but none of the family would listen when I asked for our betrothal to be ended. So I ran away to London to look for a job as a governess.'

Lord Rutherford poured himself another glass of cognac. 'What happened to you in London?'

She smiled bitterly. 'Nineteen-year-old girls without references and without teaching experience do not get offered work as a governess, my lord. The job offers I received were all of a somewhat different nature. The small income my parents had left me was administered by my cousin. He would not advance me any funds and so, within three months, my pride and ignorance had successfully brought me to the point of destitution.'

'Why were you drunk the night that I found you?'

She felt herself flush a deep, flaming red, but she forced herself to meet his gaze. 'I hadn't eaten for two days, my lord. I drank the gin to give myself courage to sell the only thing I had left to sell. You . . . you will be able to guess what I planned to do. You know the rest of my story, because you were the person who found me. I shall always be grateful, my lord, that you took me in.'

He sprang up from the chair and walked to the other side of the fireplace. 'You owe me nothing,' he said. 'God knows, you have no cause to feel grateful. For heaven's sake, Deborah, why did you never tell me the truth?'

'I was afraid you might send me back to Cousin George. Besides, what difference would it have made even if you had believed me?'

'It would certainly have been my duty to return you safely to your cousin. Naturally, I would not have asked you to marry me.'

'Then I am glad that I concealed the truth,' she said huskily. She got up from the footstool and came to stand near him. She was overwhelmingly aware of her love for him and had to fight against the urge to throw herself into his arms. 'I did not want to return to my cousin,' she said softly. 'And I . . . and I chose freely to marry you.'

'Freely!' he exclaimed. 'How can you use such a word when the only choice I offered you was starvation?'

She moved so close to him that no more than an inch or two separated her from his arms. 'I never believed that you would allow me to starve,' she said. 'I am sure that if I had refused your offer of marriage, you would have found me some other position on your estates.'

'You seriously over-estimate my goodness,' he said curtly. He drained his glass of cognac and swung away from her. 'Deborah, it is late. You should be in your bed.'

'It is lonely in my bed,' she whispered. 'And I cannot seem to fall asleep.'

There was a sudden crash as Lord Rutherford hurled his empty brandy-glass into the hearth. 'Deborah . . .' he said. 'For God's sake, go to bed.'

'I am not sleepy.'

With a harsh sigh he turned and pulled her into

his arms, kissing her passionately. 'I want you, Deborah,' he murmured against her mouth. 'I need you so much.' Her breasts were crushed tightly against him and she could feel his heart racing in unison with her own. She melted into the warmth of his embrace, the fire of her kisses fuelled by the loneliness of two months away from his arms. He pushed his hands into the long, loose strands of her hair, opening her robe so that he could press a blazing trail of kisses over her shoulders. She surrendered willingly to his lovemaking, delighting in the increasing urgency of his desire, longing for the moment when he would take her to his bed.

As suddenly as he had gathered her into his arms, he pushed her away, holding her rigidly away from him. 'This must stop,' he said harshly. 'Please go to your own bedroom, Deborah. Now!'

She swallowed the last remnant of her pride because instinct told her that he didn't really want her to leave. She moved so that her body was once again pressed closely against his and, with trembling fingers, reached inside his dressing gown to caress the naked skin of his chest.

She felt the immediate response of his body and heard the rasp of his indrawn breath, but he didn't take her into his arms. Finally, she reached up and pressed a tiny kiss on the corner of his taut mouth.

'No, we must not do this! Why won't you accept that I don't want to make love to you!' With a violent shudder, he thrust her away. Deborah, startled by the unexpected forcefulness of his move, stumbled backwards, tripping over the footstool which was just behind her. She lost her balance completely and tumbled to the floor.

'Oh my God, what have I done? My insane temper . . . My love, have I hurt you?'

She heard his agonised whisper, but for a second she was too shocked by the fall to speak. It was several moments before she caught her breath, but that was mainly because Lord Rutherford held her in his arms, gently stroking her face and hair, and not because she was in pain.

'Deborah,' he murmured again. 'Try to tell me where it hurts.'

She saw the whiteness of his face and the burning anxiety of his eyes, and her heart contracted with a surge of love. 'My lord, I am not hurt anywhere,' she said. 'Truly, I was just breathless for a second or two.'

'Your face is white,' he said.

'John . . . My lord, there is nothing to worry about. That is if you would just be kind enough to help me to get up! I have no doubt I look absurdly inelegant piled in a heap on your carpet.'

'You look beau . . .' He snapped his lips together. 'As I mentioned before, you look pale,' he said. He helped her to her feet and set her gently in the wing-chair. 'You are certain that you have suffered no ill effects?'

'I am quite certain,' she said.

The anxiety and deep concern left his face, to be replaced by the aloof expression so familiar to Deborah. 'I shall summon your maid to assist you to your room,' he said.

'My lord, there is no need. I can go alone.'

'No,' he said. 'I would never forgive myself if anything happened to you as a consequence of my uncontrollable temp . . .' He turned away from her and pulled sharply on the bell-rope. 'You will need a maid to see that you are comfortably settled,' he said.

'Perhaps you are right, my lord.'

He walked to the opposite side of the room and stood there, carefully avoiding her eyes, while they waited for the maid. Deborah looked at the rigid line of his shoulders and noted the careful blankness of his expression. A few weeks earlier she would have accepted these signs of coldness at face value. Now she knew better. She was quite certain it was not indifference which kept her husband at the other end of the room. She was sure it was not a lack of interest in her well-being which turned his knuckles white and tightened his mouth into a straight, hard line.

She greeted the maid in a state of considerable thoughtfulness, bid her husband a formal goodnight, and climbed into her bed. There were interesting plans to be made for the morning.

CHAPTER
ELEVEN

As soon as she got up the next morning, Deborah summoned the carriage and paid a call on her mother-in-law. The Dowager welcomed her warmly, although her face fell slightly when Deborah confessed that she had no intention of spending the morning at the dressmaker and didn't want to go to the shops.

The Dowager's cheerful mood was fully restored when she realised that her daughter-in-law wished to indulge in a session of family gossip. Gossip ranked only marginally below shopping in the Dowager's personal list of favourite entertainments.

Deborah had lain awake for most of the night, planning how she might tactfully broach the delicate subject of the late Lord Rutherford's manner of death. Tact, she soon discovered, was not necessary. Once safely launched upon the topic of her late husband's final illness, the Dowager overflowed with confidences.

'It was such a tragedy,' she said, fluttering a lace-trimmed handkerchief in front of her dry eyes. 'He was forced to spend his last two years in seclusion, you know, because he became so ill. He

moved to a cottage in Gloucestershire when he
realised that I could not bear to watch his suffering.
I am such a sensitive soul that I found it intolerable
to see my poor dear Julian unable to walk. In the
end, you know, he could not even see or hear very
well, so naturally I could not bring myself to visit
him at all. You can imagine, I am sure, how painful
a loving wife would find it to sit beside a husband
who cannot recognise her.' The Dowager gave a
delicate shudder and another wave of her handkerchief. 'It was all too terrible.'

'Did my husband visit his father?' Deborah
asked.

'Oh well, John, you know has altogether a different character from mine. As his wife, you must
already know that my son hasn't a sensitive bone in
his body. I have often wondered how somebody as
exquisitely delicate as I, come to produce such a
very *unemotional* child. He used to spend weeks
with his father, even when the poor man was quite
raving . . . Well, that is to say, when my dear Julian
was not at all himself and John was scarcely
more than a boy at the time. Whereas I . . .' The
Dowager shuddered again, glanced down at her dry
handkerchief, and tucked it hastily away.

'Lady Rutherford, I am sorry to bring back so
many tragic memories—particularly in view of your
tender susceptibilites—but could you please tell me
exactly what caused your husband's death?'

'Well, I'm afraid I have never quite understood
what happened. Doctors always explain things so
badly, don't you think? And then my dear Julian
took so long to die that I had to keep asking Dr

Smith when the end might come, because I wanted to stay in London for the Great Exhibition and, after all, there was no point in burying myself in the country when poor dear Julian couldn't even hear or see somebody in the same room. And really, I must say that the doctor was not at all co-operative. He paid no attention whatsoever to my sensitive nerves, even when he saw that I had hysterics every time he obliged me to walk into the sickroom.'

'You were not . . . with Lord Rutherford when he died?'

'No, but John was there, of course; he was there all along. Julian died just when I had made all arrangements to go up to London for the Season. So I was obliged to spend an entire year in Somerset, and I couldn't wear any of the new clothes I had bought and of course by the next year they were all completely out of fashion. I had one marvellous ball-gown in peach organza that I was never able to wear, and I do believe it was the most beautiful gown the local dressmaker ever made for me. I can assure you, my dear, I would never have been to survive a whole year in the country if I hadn't been such a devoted wife. But no sacrifice seemed too great if it was necessary to honour my dear Julian's memory.'

'Your devotion, Lady Rutherford, must have been truly remarkable.'

'Yes, well, I was mad for love of my dear Julian when first we met, you know. You have never seen such a handsome man, although people do tell me that my son has something of his father's air. And of course, it is only proper for a wife to spend some months in mourning, although I don't approve of these excessive displays of grief that the Queen is trying to make fashionable. Particularly since everybody knows that Prince Albert was always the most disobliging of men, which is only to be expected of a foreigner. Saxe-Coburg, I ask you! Whoever had heard of Saxe-Coburg until Albert arrived in town? And why the wretched man had to succumb to a sore throat just when we were getting ready for Christmas, I shall never know. And not only the whole of last year's Season ruined, but this year's, too. One would think that the Queen would realise she ought to come down from Balmoral by now. After all, it is two years since he died, and how long can one continue mourning for a man who spent every evening playing Bach on the organ? It is so frustrating to think that John has finally married and the Court is still in such a ridiculous state of mourning.'

'But I don't mind waiting until next year to be presented,' Deborah said soothingly. She quickly changed the subject, convinced that she would never glean accurate information about how her father-in-law died by listening to the Dowager. As the Dowager chattered on about the Prince of Wales's marriage to Princess Alexandra of Denmark, she decided that she would leave for Hinsdale Cottage on the afternoon train. She was determined to discover precisely how the previous Lord Rutherford had died, because she was becoming increasingly convinced that there was a connection between his death and her husband's reluctance to enter into a normal marriage.

She bade farewell to the Dowager with as much courtesy as she could, although she had almost bitten her tongue through on several occasions in order to keep from expressing her true opinion of her mother-in-law's comments.

When she returned home she learned that Lord Rutherford had left for a Committee session at the House of Lords. She was secretly relieved he was away, since it avoided the need for difficult explanations. She asked Margaret to pack a small valise and, having changed into a smart travelling outfit of royal blue serge, she summoned the carriage and left word with the butler that she was taking the afternoon train to Cheltenham.

Her journey was uneventful and her welcome at Hinsdale Cottage flatteringly warm. The elderly servants, with the help of the village girls, had kept the house in immaculate order, and they all vied with one another in showering attention on her. When she had changed into a simple wool dress, she summoned Mrs Potter and asked if the doctor could be sent for, explaining that she needed to consult with him immediately.

Mrs Potter's face lit up with joy. 'You be wanting the doctor, my lady? And you've chosen to come here?'

'Er . . . yes,' Deborah said, wondering why the housekeeper looked so excited. 'I particularly wished to consult with Dr Smith. Because he knows Lord Rutherford and . . . and the family so well already.'

'He's a first-rate doctor, my lady. You couldn't have made a wiser choice, I'm sure. He will see that everything goes just as it should. And when will 'is lordship be coming down from town?'

'Well . . . er . . . Lord Rutherford is very busy at the moment. But he hopes to get away before Christmas.'

'I'm sure he does, my lady. He'll be wanting to be with you, I know. I'll send Will for the doctor tonight, my lady. I've no doubt he'll be here before you finish your dinner.'

In the end, however, Deborah had to retire to bed without seeing the doctor. He had been summoned to the assistance of a desperately sick child, the housekeeper reported, and he would come to her as soon as the crisis was past.

The next morning she was still waiting for the doctor to arrive. She felt stifled by the enforced inactivity, and after breakfast she walked out to the stables, asking Will to saddle up a horse for her to ride. She refused his offer to accompany her, and set off for a gentle ramble through the countryside. 'I'm not going far,' she said. 'I shall ride south, towards the village and I would like you to come and fetch me if the doctor arrives.'

The weather was mild for December, and the sun shone with a pale yellow glow in the winter sky. Most of the trees were bare, but the hedgerows were bright with holly and the occasional stand of evergreens broke up the monotony of the horizon. After a while, she forgot that she was merely filling in time and began to take pleasure in the ride. She wandered across the fields, breathing in the crisp winter air and admiring the occasional flash of scarlet of a robin. She eventually realised that she had missed the turn-off for the village, but was quite content to continue trotting across the fields, letting the horse amble wherever he wanted to go. She glanced occasionally at the position of the sun, reassuring herself that she was travelling virtually due south. To return, she would only need to head north.

It was almost lunch-time when she first acknowledged that she was hopelessly and completely lost. She drew rein in the middle of a seemingly endless stretch of empty fields and looked back to scan the patchwork of brown tilled earth and faded grass. She wasn't sure when the sun had disappeared behind a thick band of heavy grey clouds, but now, whichever way she looked, she could spot no familiar landmark to indicate the direction of Hinsdale Cottage. There was, furthermore, no sign of human life except for a distant curl of smoke emerging from a cottage chimney. She decided regretfully that she had no choice but to ride towards the smoke.

The temperature had dropped considerably by the time she reached the cottage, and thick flakes of snow were beginning to fall as she asked the young housewife for directions back to Hinsdale Cottage. She was relieved to discover that she was no more than five miles from home, if she skirted a small copse of trees and crossed a couple of fields until she came to a stream which led straight to the cottage. She thanked the cottager and set off, shivering as a fierce gust of wind blew snow into her face. She knew the servants would be worried by her long absence, and she was cross with herself for having rambled about so carelessly. Fortunately, she hadn't galloped all morning, so the horse wasn't tired, and she urged him to a steady canter. Nevertheless, the ride home seemed unending and it was late afternoon when she saw the blaze of lights shining from the windows of Hinsdale Cottage. She couldn't remember ever seeing a more welcome sight.

She rode right into the yard, too weary to take her mount to the stable. She didn't have to summon Will. As she pulled the horse to a halt, the kitchen door was thrown open and Lord Rutherford stormed out. He was dressed in riding-clothes and was followed by a bevy of servants, who set up a chorus of clucks and delighted cries as they hurried across the courtyard behind their master.

'Thank the Lord, my lady! You're safe!' the housekeeper exclaimed. 'You aren't hurt, are you, my lady?'

'No, I am quite well, just a little chilled.'

'Where have you been?' Lord Rutherford demanded coldly, cutting across the servants' babble of questions. 'I have just finished organising search-parties to set off in pursuit of you. Half the men in the village have been obliged to turn out of their homes in order to come and look for you.'

'I was lost,' she said. 'I am very sorry to have caused so much trouble.' Her voice was hoarse with exhaustion, but his expression did not soften. On the contrary, he looked excessively grim as he turned to summon Will to his side. 'Hold Morning Glory, please,' he said and immediately reached up to lift her out of the saddle.

'My lord, I can walk,' she protested, but he paid no heed to her words as he carried her across the yard into the house. 'Give the villagers some cake and hot cider before they go home,' he instructed the housekeeper. 'And please offer them my sincere thanks for their willingness to turn out on such a cold afternoon.' He spoke again to the groom. 'Get Dr Smith here as quickly as you can, Will.'

He marched into the drawing-room and set Deborah down in front of the fire. 'You are frozen,' he said. 'Didn't it occur to you that people would be worried about you? Why did you ride off alone when you are unfamiliar with the countryside? Have you no sense? Good God, I don't know what Will was thinking of, allowing you to take out Morning Glory! It's a miracle you weren't thrown. He is far too high-spirited for a woman.'

'I am a competent rider,' she said. 'And I never allowed him to go faster than a sedate canter.'

'Sedate!' he exclaimed bitterly as he tugged at the bellrope. 'You don't know the meaning of the word! You are a constant torment to me. How could you ride out at this time of year without even a servant to keep you company? Are you trying to give yourself an inflammation of the lungs? Was *that* your object?' He tugged again at the bell. 'Where are those wretched servants? You need a hot drink if you are to avoid a severe chill. I trust the doctor will get here soon and recommend some way to protect you from the consequences of your own folly.' He swung around to face her, his expression still furious. 'And, while we are discussing your follies, I would like to know by what right you

decided to leave London without so much as a word
to me. I do not expect, madam, to discover your
whereabouts from my own butler. Even if you care
nothing for my feelings, you might give some
thought to the propriety of your behaviour.
Perhaps, in future, you will bear in mind that a
certain measure of decorum is expected of you. I
would like you to remember you are now Lady
Rutherford—*my wife*.'

'How could I ever forget?' Deborah said wearily.
Her damp clothes clung to her body, chilling her to
the bone. She hadn't eaten since breakfast, and
Lord Rutherford had arrived before she could
speak privately to the doctor. To her chagrin, the
tears she had fought off for hours suddenly welled
up and began to trickle down her cheeks. It was all
so useless. The doctor would never speak freely to
her with Lord Rutherford around. She was never
going to discover the truth about the old baron's
illness. Her husband was never going to admit that
he loved her. A wave of nausea clutched at her
throat and she swayed, momentarily overcome by
dizziness.

In an instant she was swept off her feet and into
Lord Rutherford's arms. 'Oh, sweetheart, I didn't
mean a word of it,' he groaned. 'Deborah, you are
so pale! I'm sorry I shouted at you, but I have been
out of my mind with worry ever since I learned you
had left London.' He carried her to the sofa,
anxiously rippling open the fastenings of her riding-
habit, chafing her hands solicitously and pouring
out a whispered torrent of apologies and endear-
ments. 'Deborah, my love, I have treated you so

badly, but I never meant to be such an ogre. Oh God, where is that damned doctor?' He stroked her hair, tenderly pushing it away from her forehead. 'Please answer me, my dearest, I can't bear it if you are ill. Why won't you speak to me!'

Deborah's moment of faintness passed as quickly as it came. She decided, however, that there was no need to inform her husband of this fact provided he continued to hold her in his arms and murmured passionate words of love into her ears. She moaned as realistically as she could manage without ruining her portrayal of fragile femininity, and then allowed her body to droop pathetically against the strength of her husband's chest. She hoped he wouldn't notice that a strange, feverish heat had entirely dissipated her original icy coldness. She was surprised that he hadn't detected the erratic racing of her heart as it beat against his own.

There were, unfortunately, limits to her powers of dissembling. She had just decided that she was going to have to regain consciousness (perhaps she could allow him to kiss her one more time before she opened her eyes?), when the housekeeper bustled into the drawing-room, announcing the arrival of the doctor.

'About time too!' Lord Rutherford exclaimed, springing to his feet. 'Dr Smith, my wife has fainted and nothing I can do seems to revive her!'

Deborah hastily gave another of her artistic moans, and did her best to portray a lady slowly regaining command of her senses. She raised herself delicately on one elbow. She pressed a fluttering hand against her forehead in an exquisite gesture of bewilderment. 'Oh dear!' she sighed. 'Where am I? What has happened to me?'

The doctor's gaze flicked over her with disconcerting shrewdness. 'His lordship was reviving you from a fainting fit,' he said. 'It seems that his methods work admirably, for I've never seen so fine a blush of colour on the cheeks of a young woman who's just recovering from a swoon.'

The blush he referred to darkened by several shades. 'I . . . er . . . My husband . . . er . . .' Deborah's explanations ground to an unconvincing halt, and she was greatly relieved when the doctor turned away and shut the door firmly behind the housekeeper. He walked briskly to the sofa. 'Now what's all this I heard about you, my lady? Riding out alone in this cold weather and in your condition, too? That wasn't very sensible, now was it? No wonder you felt faint.'

He put the back of his hand against her brow, then grunted non-committally. Lord Rutherford paced up and down the room, his face drawn with anxiety, while the doctor completed his examination. 'What is your opinion?' he enquired as soon as the doctor finished. 'Has my wife contracted any fever? Is she . . . is she seriously ill?'

'Apart from the fact that she has spent too long in the saddle on a snowy day, there is nothing at all wrong with Lady Rutherford,' the doctor answered somewhat testily. 'She obviously has an excellent constitution. A good meal and a sound night's sleep should put all to rights. However, my lady, I must say that I don't approve of you riding out alone in your condition. I take the privilege of a physician who has served this family for many years, and I must inform you that you were taking an unnecessary risk with the health and well-being of your unborn baby. We do not want a prospective Lord Rutherford arriving months before he is due.'

His words fell into a silence that seemed to stretch out almost for ever. Lord Rutherford suddenly spun on his heel and came to Deborah's side. He sat beside her, holding her hands, his face contorted with anguish. 'Tell me it isn't true!' he pleaded. 'That night . . . after we had been to the Opera . . . I prayed this wouldn't happen.' He brushed his hand over his eyes. 'Oh, God, Deborah, I can't find words to tell you how sorry I am.'

She kept her eyes fixed on the lean, strong fingers that enfolded her hands. 'Why do you apologise so profusely for such a natural event? We are . . . we are married, after all.'

'There are reasons,' he said, very low. 'Deborah, I have—I have not lied to you, but neither have I told you the whole truth about myself.' He turned to look at the doctor, Deborah's hand still held tight within his grasp. 'Are you sure, Dr Smith? There is no doubt in your mind that my wife is going to have a baby?'

The doctor surveyed them both thoughtfully. 'I am sorry, my lady, if I have blurted out news that you wished to confide to his lordship at some more appropriate time. The housekeeper sent me a message yesterday, informing me that you were with child and had travelled down from London to consult me. I regret, my lord, that I assumed because of this message that you were already aware of your wife's condition.'

Deborah found it ironic that Mrs Potter's unwarranted leaping to conclusions had precipitated precisely the discussion she herself had despaired of bringing about. She glanced at her husband and saw that his face was devoid of all trace of colour and, for a moment, she was afraid that *he* might be in danger of fainting. She touched her hand to his cheek in a gentle caress. 'Do you mind so very much?' she asked softly. 'I have suspected the truth for some weeks but I could never find the right moment to tell you about it.'

'My dear,' he said huskily. 'It's not that I mind. In many ways, the knowledge that you are carrying my child . . . I wish . . . Oh God! What in heaven's name am I to do?' He got up from the sofa and walked slowly to the window, parting the heavy velvet drapes and staring out into the snowy darkness of the night. He was, if anything, greyer than before when he finally turned and began to speak. 'Dr Smith, what are we to do? You know the truth about my family. For God's sake help me. Tell me what I should do now, I beg you.'

'As soon as I have left, I would recommend that you request some soup and hot milk for her ladyship. I would then further recommend that you thank the Almighty for blessing you with the promise of children so early in your marriage. I anticipate no particular problems with this pregnancy, none at all. I am happy to say that Lady Rutherford appears to me to be a wonderfully healthy young woman.'

'It is not my wife's health which concerns me,' Lord Rutherford said tightly. 'It is my own.'

'Ah! So *that* is what's bothering you.' The doctor was silent for a few moments and Deborah was convinced that she saw a gleam of compassion soften his normally matter-of-fact expression. 'Well, my lord,' he said finally. 'I am happy to reassure you. Your health is excellent, and quite up to the demands likely to be placed upon it over the next few months. As a mere prospective father, you know, you will not be called upon to perform any very arduous duties. In the circumstances, therefore, undue concern about the state of your own health is somewhat irrelevant.'

'You are determined not to understand me,' Lord Rutherford said tersely. 'You know that I am not worried about my present health. I am worried about the future, damn you! I am worried about the day when my headaches no longer torment me for a day or so and then disappear. I am worried about the day when they remain with me permanently, driving me mad with the pain.'

'Like your father, perhaps?' the doctor said quietly.

'Yes!' Lord Rutherford shouted. 'Like my father! How long do you think it will be, Dr Smith, before I, too, lose my sight and my hearing? How long do you estimate I still have before I start to rant and scream and rage because I cannot stand the pain?' He sank despairingly into a chair. 'And how long before the poor unfortunate child I have procreated learns about the fate that will one day overtake him?'

'A very long time, I should think,' said the doctor calmly. 'I told you when I was here a few weeks ago, my lord, that you do not suffer from the same disease as your father. The late Lord Rutherford developed a malignant growth on the brain and that growth eventually killed him.'

'And do you expect me to believe that he never suffered from painful headaches? Have you forgotten my father's violent bursts of temper during the last months of his life? Have you forgotten the days when he was driven mad by the pain?'

'They were most distressing,' the doctor agreed. 'But I repeat, my lord, that such outbursts were a result of pressure on his brain, caused by the growth that killed him. You have no grounds for expecting any similar fate to overtake you.'

Lord Rutherford stared into the embers of the fire. 'You are forgetting one important fact,' he said. 'What of my own headaches, which have already caused me to black out with pain? Why do you try to protect my feelings by lying about my fate? I should never have married. I should never have allowed myself to father a child. The time has come for us to speak bluntly to one another. Why don't you admit that my blood . . . my blood is tainted with a hereditary affliction . . .'

Dr Smith sighed in exasperation. 'Because your blood is not tainted with *anything*,' he said.

'Yes, it is!' Deborah exclaimed, sitting up straight on the sofa. 'It is tainted with a vastly excessive dose of obstinacy. You insist that your headaches are symptoms of some dreadful disease, even though the doctor has told you they are nothing of the sort. My mother suffered from sick headaches just like yours, and her physician said they were caused chiefly by the tensions inevitable in the life of a great soprano. Dr Smith has said that you suffer from headaches because you worry too much and not because of the onset of insanity. Why won't you believe him?'

The doctor glanced at her approvingly. 'Lady Rutherford is quite right, you know, my lord. The headaches from which you suffer are called migraines, and they have been recorded in medical history since the time of the Ancient Greeks. There is no evidence to show that the pain will have any effect upon your natural lifespan. Indeed, I have recently read an article which suggests that the pain of migraine headaches becomes less severe as the sufferer gets older.' He crossed the room and shook Lord Rutherford's hand with the affection of an old family friend. 'Come, my lord, put these worries behind you. I am looking forward to seeing you surrounded by a clutch of boisterous children who will keep you far too busy to permit time for brooding about a past which is well and truly over. I will now bid you and her ladyship goodnight. Lady Rutherford will want to change into some dryer and more comfortable clothes. Don't bother to summon Jenkins, I can certainly find my own way out.'

When the doctor had left, an awkward silence descended upon the drawing-room. Lord Rutherford cleared his throat nervously once or twice, then finally came and sat beside Deborah on the sofa. 'It seems I am for ever needing to beg your forgiveness,' he said. 'What can I say except that I am deeply—desperately—sorry that I took advantage of your innocence without telling you the truth about myself. Or at least what I imagined to be the truth.'

'Yes,' she said softly. 'I wish that you had told me the truth.'

'I promise you, Deborah, that I will never again take advantage of your sweetly trusting and innocent nature.'

'My sweetly innocent nature! Oh—er—yes, yes of course . . .'

'I shall never again allow temptation to overcome my obligations to you. I shall not so much as enter your bedroom, I swear it.'

She sighed deeply and fell back against the cushions of the sofa. 'How *excessively* noble of you, my lord.' She allowed another whispered sigh to escape from her lips as she peered at him through half-closed lashes.

'My dearest . . . that is to say, Deborah, aren't you feeling well? You sound so weak, so exhausted. Perhaps you should go to your bedroom right away. I will ask the housekeeper to bring you some dinner on a tray.'

Deborah managed to inject another convincing quaver into her voice. 'You are probably right,' she said. 'I think I should lie down on my bed but . . . but unfortunately, I feel so frail. I don't think I am strong enough to walk upstairs. Being *enceinte*, you know . . .' She allowed her voice to trail off into a feeble murmur.

'I shall carry you upstairs, my dear. You must rest and take the greatest care of yourself. One has only to look at you to see how delicate your constitution must be.'

Deborah snapped her lips together just in time to stop herself pointing out that the doctor had commented on the robustness of her health scarcely five minutes earlier. She collapsed with convincing helplessness against Lord Rutherford's chest, clasping her arms around his neck and twining her fingers into the thickeness of his hair. She nestled her cheek closely against his shirt-front and was delighted to hear the quickened pace of his breathing. His difficulty was not caused, she was certain, by the effort of carrying her up a shallow flight of stairs.

Lord Rutherford laid her gently on the bed. 'Will you be all right now?'

'Actually, I think I ought to get undressed. Dr Smith suggested that I should get into something more comfortable.'

'I shall send up one of the maids to assist you,' he replied, striding determinedly towards the door.

'John, please don't go!' He paused, one foot in the hall, and looked back at her. Deborah did her very best to appear pale and wan, which was somewhat difficult when her pulses were racing with a feverish, exultant excitement. 'My lord, I don't think I am strong enough to cope with half-trained village girls just at the moment. Could you . . . could *you* help me to undress?'

Lord Rutherford turned pale. He swallowed convulsively. 'Deborah, I'm sure that a maid . . .'

'I would prefer you to undress me,' she said

huskily, speaking the truth for almost the first time
since the doctor had left.

Lord Rutherford nervously approached the bed
and with stiff, jerky movements began to unfasten
the buttons of her riding-habit. By the time her
skirt and jacket were safely removed, his mouth
was drawn into a tight line of repression and his
eyes were dark with frustrated passion. He unbut-
toned her blouse. 'Surely you can manage to take
off the rest,' he said curtly.

'But you are doing so well,' she murmured. 'Why
don't you allow me to remove your jacket, and then
we could both be comfortable together?' She
slipped off his jacket without giving him any chance
to reply, then ran her hands enticingly over his
body. He said nothing. In fact, from the rigid
grimness of his expression, she judged him to be
well past the point of exchanging pleasantries. She
began slowly to unfasten the buttons of his silk-
lined waistcoat. When the waistcoat had joined his
jacket and her riding-habit on the floor, she pushed
her hands beneath his shirt, smiling with secret
pleasure when she felt his body shudder against her
palms.

'Deborah,' he groaned. 'We must not . . . Your
condition! My promise to you . . . I have broken
my word so many times.'

She leaned her head against his shoulder, stroking his cheek in a loving caress. 'But you never
asked me if I wanted you to make all those silly
promises,' she said, reaching up to kiss the taut
corner of his mouth. 'As it happens, I have only one
promise that I require you to make to me and in my

delicate condition I dare say it would be fatal if you decided to refuse me.'

'Anything!'

She looked straight into his eyes. 'I want you to love me for the rest of my life,' she said.

'That is very easily promised. Deborah, I love you more than I ever thought it possible to love any woman. I wish I knew how . . . there is no way to show you how much I love you.'

She thrust her body a little bit closer to his, and allowed her fingers to trail slowly across his lips. 'Oh,' she said softly. 'I'm sure you are wrong. There must be many ways you could show me how much you love me.' She unfastened the last of his shirt-buttons and lifted her mouth so that it hovered only a breath away from his. 'Are you still convinced there is no way to show me how much you love me?'

'But you are faint with exhaustion!'

'You are wrong, my lord,' she whispered. 'If I am faint, it is because I have been waiting so long for you to kiss me.'

He pulled her into his arms and kissed her hungrily, and she returned the kiss with a passion that matched his own. After several breathless minutes, he tore himself out of her arms and subjected her to a ruthless, piercing scrutiny. 'You, madam wife, were no more on the verge of fainting than I was!'

'That is true,' she admitted humbly.

'There was absolutely no necessity for me to carry you upstairs. You were perfectly capable of walking by yourself.'

'That is also true,' she said, hanging her head.

'There is, in fact, no reason whatsoever why you should remain in bed.'

She looked up and he saw that her eyes were alight with warmth and love and laughter. 'That, my lord, is not true at all. There is an excellent reason for me to remain in bed.'

'I cannot imagine what it might be.'

'You make a shocking liar, my lord, but if you will lean a little closer, I will try to help you increase the scope of your imagination.'

The laughter faded from his eyes. 'I love you, Deborah,' he said.

'I love you, too,' she replied, and the rest of her words were swept away, lost for ever in the passion of her husband's embrace.

THE END

Mills & Boon

Your chance to step into the past Take 2 Books FREE

Discover a world long vanished. An age of chivalry and intrigue, powerful desires and exotic locations. Read about true love found by soldiers and statesmen, princesses and serving girls. All written as only Mills & Boon's top-selling authors know how. Become a regular reader of Mills & Boon Masquerade Historical Romances and enjoy 4 superb, new titles every two months, plus a whole range of special benefits: your very own personal membership card entitles you to a regular free newsletter packed with recipes, competitions, exclusive book offers plus other bargain offers and big cash savings.

AND an Introductory FREE GIFT for YOU. Turn over the page for details.

**Fill in and send this coupon back today
and we will send you**

2 Introductory
Historical Romances
FREE

At the same time we will reserve a subscription to
Mills & Boon Masquerade Historical Romances for
you. Every two months you will receive Four new,
superb titles delivered direct to your door. You
don't pay extra for delivery. Postage and packing is
always completely free. There is no obligation or
commitment – you only receive books for as long as
you want to.

**Just fill in and post the coupon today to MILLS & BOON
READER SERVICE, FREEPOST, P.O. BOX 236, CROYDON,
SURREY CR9 9EL.**

**Please Note:- READERS iN SOUTH AFRICA write to
Mills & Boon, Postbag X3010,
Randburg 2125, S. Africa.**

- -

FREE BOOKS CERTIFICATE

**To: Mills & Boon Reader Service, FREEPOST, P.O. Box 236,
Croydon, Surrey CR9 9EL.**

Please send me, free and without obligation, two Masquerade Historical Romances, and
reserve a Reader Service Subscription for me. If I decide to subscribe I shall receive,
following my free parcel of books, four new Masquerade Historical Romances every two
months for £5.00, post and packing free. If I decide not to subscribe, I shall write to you
within 10 days. The free books are mine to keep in any case. I understand that I may cancel
my subscription at any time simply by writing to you. I am over 18 years of age.

Please write in BLOCK CAPITALS.

Signature _____

Name _____

Address _____

_____ Post code _____

SEND NO MONEY — TAKE NO RISKS.

Please don't forget to include your Postcode.

Remember, postcodes speed delivery. Offer applies in UK only and is not valid
to present subscribers. Mills & Boon reserve the right to exercise discretion in
granting membership. If price changes are necessary you will be notified.
4M Offer expires December 24th 1984.

EP9M